Contact
HIGH

TORI ROSS

Contact High

TORI ROSS

Copyright © 2023 by Tori Ross

All rights reserved.

The characters and events portrayed in this book are fictitious. Any similarity to real persons, living or dead, is coincidental and not intended by the author.

No part of this book may be reproduced, or stored in any retrieval system, or transmitted in any form or by any means, electronic, mechanical photocopying, recording, or otherwise, without express written permission of the publisher.

All main characters are age 18+

Cover Design: Coffin Print Designs

Edited by: Deb Kuntzman

Author Note

On November 8, 2022, the citizens of Missouri legalized recreational marijuana for adults twenty-one and over. Since it was legalized, the legislature enacted several rules surrounding the growth and sales of the substance. There are rules on packaging, growing only certain amounts, and you can only make one purchase a day, tracked by having the back of your ID scanned. There are so many rules and regulations surrounding the legalization, that I was not able to keep up with them in writing this book. I started this book in January of 2023 before the legalization took effect and when the rules were still being sorted, so I may have a few things wrong. Please note that I did my best with the information I had at the time. I did research some police procedurals, but not everything is correct because I needed Liam and Chase to do certain things to advance the plot.

Please read the trigger warnings. If you have a cancer patient in your life, please note that Liam's mother is fighting cancer. Please also note that there is a chapter that has strangulation and gun violence directed toward a police officer. If you are a victim of strangulation or gun violence, please skip that chapter and move to the next. It will not inhibit your ability to enjoy the story.

Contact High Playlist

Fight for Your Right – The Beastie Boys
Levitating – Dua Lipa
Another Brick in the Wall – Pink Floyd
Shots – LMFAO, Little John
Love Game – Lady Gaga
Blow – Kesha
Graveyard – Halsey
Only Happy When It Rains – Garbage
Bad Reputation – Joan Jett
Shut Up and Drive – Rhianna
Brutal – Olivia Rodrigo
Karma – Taylor Swift

You can find the entire playlist on Spotify named as *Contact High Playlist*.

Contents

1. Chapter 1 — 1
2. Chapter 2 — 9
3. Chapter 3 — 16
4. Chapter 4 — 23
5. Chapter 5 — 30
6. Chapter 6 — 36
7. Chapter 7 — 44
8. Chapter 8 — 53
9. Chapter 9 — 61
10. Chapter 10 — 70
11. Chapter 11 — 79
12. Chapter 12 — 86
13. Chapter 13 — 93
14. Chapter 14 — 100

15.	Chapter 15	108
16.	Chapter 16	116
17.	Chapter 17	124
18.	Chapter 18	132
19.	Chapter 19	138
20.	Chapter 20	147
21.	Chapter 21	155
22.	Chapter 22	161
23.	Chapter 23	167
24.	Chapter 24	173
25.	Chapter 25	183
26.	Chapter 26	189
27.	Chapter 27	196
28.	Chapter 28	203
29.	Chapter 29	210
30.	Epilogue	216
About the Author		223
Acknowledgements		224

Chapter 1

LORELEI

"What's in it?" the older woman at the window asks, pushing her glasses back onto her long nose and simultaneously looking at the brownie like it's an insect to be squashed. She looks about sixty, and I bet she's never purchased a weed brownie from a food truck before. Hell, she's probably never had a weed brownie at all.

"The strain relaxes you. Mellows you out. Perfect for a jazz concert, wouldn't you say?" I nod toward the gate entrance to the outdoor concert arena.

People have been covertly smoking joints in the lawn seats here for decades. They've used covert ways of getting past security, shoving joints into their shoes and blowing the smoke through blowtubes made of toilet paper rolls and dryer sheets.

But it's legal now.

The good citizens of Missouri voted to legalize marijuana under three ounces and decriminalize possession charges last year. As soon as the permit process opened, I applied for my cultivation and seller permit. While other sellers flocked to the shop strategy at the borders of surrounding states, I went for something a little more niche. I now have my own food truck that specializes in edibles and caters to event goers, complete with my own patented cannabutter with a few secret infusion extras. Depending on what I'm baking with it, the butter can also have tea, coffee, cardamon, and cinnamon infused with it. Mostly cinnamon. In fact, my most popular cannabutter is simply butter, marijuana, and cinnamon. But people marvel at it like I invented the light bulb.

There are still rules, permits, red tape to jump over, and hoops to dodge, but it can be consumed on private property. Thankfully, the concert arena owner is weed friendly, and the land is privately owned. The owner, Buddy Wilkens, was more than happy to let me park my food truck, Lorelei's Blissful Baked Goods, on a small patch of grass between the entrance and parking lot.

"If this were a Metallica concert, there'd be a different strain in it. I have to know my customers." I chuckle at my own joke and stiffen when the lady doesn't laugh.

I guess she's *that* kind of customer. Too bad she can't report me to the police any longer, and I smile with the knowledge. Then again, she's probably here to hold up the line. I get those every now and then. People who hate marijuana and want to keep people from buying it any way they can.

"Can I help you?" I ask the next customer in line, a younger bald man with a pierced nose. My kind of person.

I finger my own nose stud, remembering the terrible infection I got. I thought it would make me look edgy for the customers when I started selling a few months back, even though you have to be close to see it since it's so small. Kailee, my employee that helps on the weekends and substitute teaches during the day, did it herself.

Don't let an untrained person pierce your nose. Lesson learned.

I catch a glimpse of Kailee out of the corner of my eye as she works at the back of the truck, stirring the fudge ingredients and donning an oven mitt before taking a tray of cookies from the truck oven.

"Yeah, I'll take a brownie and one of the mint cupcakes," the man says. "Do you have any vanilla cupcakes?"

Amateur. My shoulders slouch, disappointed that I still get asked about vanilla baked goods, but I still smile. I never miss an opportunity to educate about edibles. "Actually, there's a reason that people bake marijuana into things like chocolate or brownies," I say, shrugging as the older woman stomps off. The man steps closer, his eyebrows raised like we're in a chemistry lab and I'm explaining something cool.

We kind of are. I mean, I always loved *Breaking Bad*, but making my own cannabutter for baked goods took some trial and error, and I ruined more than a couple slow cookers in the process. The recipes took months to be tweaked into something that tasted good and got people high.

"The key is saturated butter," I say, grabbing a stick of the butter from the mini fridge next to the register. "Cannabutter. You can't just sprinkle weed into a batter. You have to infuse the butter by melting it with leaves, removing the leaves, and letting the butter solidify again. When the butter is infused, it's greenish, sometimes darker green. It really doesn't work well in white baked goods. I mean, you can have it in vanilla, and it tastes good. People just don't like eating green-tinged baked goods," I explain, waffling my head side-to-side. "Well, unless it's St. Patrick's Day."

"Whoa. So cool. Did you figure that out yourself?"

I chuckle. "No. Some dude taught me how to do it in college. This is how it's been done for decades, my friend. I grow my own plants and infuse my own butter that I use in the truck. You can go to my website and buy your own to use at home."

He gets his phone out and takes a picture of the side of my truck with my website information under the truck name, and I hand him an environmentally friendly paper bag with his pastries, wrapped in their wrappers to show what strain it is, as required by law. "Enjoy the show."

He waves, and the next person approaches. A fifty-something woman with purple hair adjusts noise-canceling headphones over her ears and stands on her tiptoes to look at my menu. "So fucking cool," she mumbles. "Do you only do this for concerts?" she asks, her eyes moving to the case containing the wrapped peanut butter fudge and the case of chocolate chunk cookies.

"I do birthday parties." I lean over the ledge and hand her my business card.

"Shut the front fucking door," she says, looking at it.

"The only rule is that the birthday has to be on private property. It can't be a park or something. I usually back the truck into a driveway."

"Awesome. I'll take two," she says, nodding to the case with the fudge squares.

Customers come and go over the next hour as they purchase their edibles before the show starts. I run out of business cards and make a mental note to order more. Even better, I run out of most pastries. Kailee checks the fridge and tsks. "We're out of everything except for three mint chocolate cupcakes. Want to have a good time?" she asks, waggling her eyebrows. We're not above eating a leftover pastry at the end of the night.

"That still leaves one."

"I'll take it," a voice says from the window.

Turning around, my insides freeze. I usually can't see people if I'm not right at the window, but I can see his head and shoulders. Either he's incredibly tall, or he's on a step stool. He's wearing aviators like he's a pilot. No, police officer. He reeks of cop, but fuck me, he's hot as hell.

"Can I help you?" I smile, sauntering to the window.

He returns the smile, but I can spot a fake smile a mile away. "What do we have here?" he asks, nodding to the lone cupcake I'm holding in my hand. "I couldn't help but overhear you wanting to have some leftovers. It's illegal to imbibe in marijuana and drive."

"We usually wait until we get home before we eat the leftovers, mister..."

"Lane. *Officer* Lane. Drug task force." His smile disappears from his face, and I miss it.

His full, bowed lips settle into a straight line that doesn't suit him. He runs his hands over the stubble coating his cheeks, but he doesn't touch the wavy hair on his head. Aren't cops supposed to have buzz cuts? His dark brown hair curls at the ends just over his ears, and I lament that he doesn't touch it. I'd like to know how it waves when he's frustrated.

"Would you like the last one, Officer Lane?" I say, holding up the cupcake inside its plastic container with the strain sticker on it and the date it was made. "If it's your birthday, I can put a candle on it."

Shit. Did I just bat my eyelashes when I said that? I blink again, hoping to pass off that I have something stuck in my long, fake eyelashes so he won't know I'm thinking about how I'd like to undo his pants and check out his night stick.

I lean against the metal window frame and look down. Yep, totally sexy. Tight-fitting dark jeans and a simple black t-shirt that stretches across those sexy shoulders. His badge sits in his waistband, and he pushes his sunglasses up his nose with his middle finger, a slow indication that he really isn't impressed with my behavior.

I sigh and hold out the decorative paper plate holding the cupcake and smile. "Be cool. Live a little," I whisper, mentally acknowledging that I sound like the stereotypical drug pusher that jumps out at middle schoolers from behind a tree.

"I prefer not to. I just saw this while I was driving by and had to give it a look. I assume you have all the proper permits and licenses?" he asks, patting the side of the truck like he's taking it for a test drive. He squints at the sign indicating lunches. "Do you serve food besides pastries?"

"No, sir. That's leftover from the last owner. I need to get it replaced, but it's stuck on there tight, and it looks tacky when I try to paint over it."

He clears his throat again. "I'll ask again. Do you have the correct permits?"

"Of course."

Kailee slides up to my side and looks down at him. "Damn," she whispers under her breath. "Is he going to handcuff you? If not, can he cuff me?" I step on her foot, and she grunts. "I'm just saying," she whispers before walking away.

"That's disgusting," he says, ignoring Kailee and nodding at the gorgeous cupcake in front of him.

"What's wrong with it?"

"It's drugs. I hate drugs. I hate people that push drugs."

My face reddens, and my nostrils flare. "Officer Lane, do you drink beer?"

He scoffs and puts his hands on his hips. "Sure."

"Technically, alcohol is a drug. So is a bottle of cold medicine. It's in the usage." I tilt my head and put on my most condescending snarl. "Whether you like it or not, the voters of this state legalized marijuana for recreational use on private property and with the proper packaging. I park on private property and have all appropriate seller licenses. I've paid my fees to the state, I don't drive while eating my own product, sell only to people before the show, check ID, and always have under the allowed amount on the truck. I even have a transportation license," I say, tapping the framed piece of paper behind my Square reader. "Regarding the three ounces rule, in case you didn't know, three ounces is actually a fuck ton of weed and even less when we're talking cannabutter. If you have a problem with any of this, you can take it up with all 1,089,326 citizens that voted to legitimize this business."

He backs away from the order area and looks at the side of my truck, then back to me. Fuck, I'd love to see what color his eyes are under those aviators. I bet they're blue. No. Probably green. To keep from thinking about his eyes, I push the cupcake to him. "Here. On the house."

"I'm going to take this to the office and make sure it's just THC in there. Are you adding any other drugs to it?"

Laughter bubbles from my chest. "Are you fucking kidding me right now?"

"I'm an officer of the law, ma'am. I expect you to be respectful when you answer my questions."

"Well, Officer Lane, if I'm being questioned about illegal activity, I'd be happy to answer your questions with an attorney present. As I am operating on private property in a perfectly legal capacity, I'll answer any harassing questions the way I please."

He pulls his phone out and takes a picture of the truck, including my website information. Normally, I'd be happy someone was interested, but my gut tells me I haven't heard the last of him.

"I'll be watching you," he says, pointing his finger at me. I half expect him to wag his finger like he's scolding a child. "This is wrong, immoral, and I'll make sure you toe the law."

He turns and walks away, my cupcake in his hand like it's a dead animal he's trying not to touch. He takes long strides away from the truck, and I watch his chiseled ass muscles clench as he walks. My mouth feels like cotton, but I clear my throat and try to think of something witty to put him in his place.

"I do birthday parties!"

Chapter 2

LIAM

"I hate my own mother fucking generation," I grunt, swinging my legs onto my desk and blowing on the cup of coffee in my hands. "They'll weasel out of and into anything under the guise of being a fucking entrepreneur, won't they?"

My partner, Chase Barnett, grunts over his own cup of coffee across from me and ignores me as he looks between an open manilla folder and his laptop screen. Built like a brick shit house with curly blonde hair, my partner gets more pussy than a cat shelter, and it's how we ended up as partners. The other detectives call us Hot and Hotter, and we got assigned on undercover cases together for our ability to get the drug girlfriends talking and ingrain ourselves as the dealer's drinking buddies. We like to argue over which one of us is Hot and which one of us is Hotter, even asking women on the force. So far, we've heard mixed results.

I was innocently driving to the station for my late afternoon shift when I caught the name of the food truck out of the corner of my eye. I thought it was a regular cupcake truck and thought I'd check it out, only to realize the cupcakes and other baked goods were laced with the devil's lawn. What kind of loser sells drugs out of a truck?

I certainly wasn't expecting *her*. She seemed like someone I'd swipe right for on Tinder, and I can't help but think that blond hair would look fantastic in my lap as I comb my hands through it.

"Are you going to eat the cupcake?" Chase asks without looking up from his folder. He squints over a mugshot of a meth dealer we've been trying to bust for six months. "If you aren't going to eat it, I'll take it home."

"You will fucking not."

"Why not? It's legal now. It's like having a beer after work."

"Like hell," I grumble. I pick up the cupcake, hold it in my palm, and point to it with my other hand like the cupcake is a prize on *Wheel of Fortune*. "If you eat this cupcake, it'll send you down a dark and dirty road. Tonight, you'll lick this frosting off, thinking it tastes good and it's just a quick bit of fun. Next week, you'll be licking some guy named Dale's frenulum for a hit of meth. You know this stuff is the gateway to hell."

Chase rolls his eyes and looks back to the folder. "You're not just the drug police. You're the fun police. I think you should eat it and chill the fuck out."

I look at the cupcake and its gorgeous creamy green frosting. As I stare at it, a lone chocolate chip piece falls onto the bottom of the container as if calling to me like a siren song. If there was a perfect cupcake in the world, I imagine it would look like this and be baked by a goddess with long blond hair and a smattering of freckles across the bridge of her nose. "I'm not going to eat it. This is evidence."

Chase laughs. "Evidence of what? Genius ambition?"

It's my turn to laugh. "Since when did you start calling drug sellers genius?"

He finally looks up at me, grinning. "You have to admit some of them are smart as fuck. But is this one really a drug crime lord?"

He's not wrong. Most of the suppliers and upper-level dealers we investigate are candidates for Mensa, and it's usually the guys and gals with the lower IQs that are the ones that get caught and take the fall for the big fish. I've been a drug task force agent for the county for the past five years, and in that same time, I can count on one hand the number of big dealers and suppliers we've caught. Those busts are few and far between compared to the routine traffic stops and random house raids that only yield a couple of low-level sellers tweaked out on their own product.

"Just because she doesn't look like a drug dealer, doesn't mean she isn't. You know that looks can be deceiving."

His smirk gets bigger. "I didn't say anything about how she looks. Exactly what does she look like?" he asks, squinting.

I shrug and sit up in my chair, swinging my feet under my desk and opening my own laptop to get to work for the evening. "Like nothing," I scoff. "Just a girl."

Chase bites his lip. Fuck, he's on to me. "Let me guess. Pink."

"What's pink?"

"The truck." He holds up his hands and makes a waxing motion. "I'm getting a 'pink curlicues and light green accents on a white background' vibe. She's about thirty with red hair that pops against a pink apron. How'd I do?"

"Blond. About twenty-four or twenty-five. Robin egg blue accents. The apron was white."

"But I nailed the rest?"

"Go fuck yourself."

He giggles and takes a sip of coffee, slurping it loudly since it's still balls hot. "She was pretty, huh?"

"Not even a little." The lie is almost painful as it rolls off my tongue. I understand why they call it a forked tongue now. My tongue nearly splits in half saying that whopper. Fuck, she was pretty. Like...I can't get her out of my mind pretty.

I'll be damned before I publicly admit a drug seller is pretty, though.

"She *was* pretty," Chase pushes.

"Pretty like your mom coming on my dick last night," I mumble, logging into my system and giving the illusion that I'm working hard and definitely not thinking about the hot woman with the weed truck.

"Going with the mom jokes, huh? She must have been really hot to get you so riled up. If she's the girl version of that pretty cupcake, maybe I'll have to check out that food truck."

I open my mouth to respond that I don't want Chase near that gorgeous drug dealer just as my desk phone lights up. I give Chase the finger and press the answer button. "Lane," I grunt in my best cop voice.

"Liam?"

I pick up the handset so Chase can't hear my conversation. We usually take phone calls so the other can hear it in case it's an informant. But Chase doesn't need to hear my phone call with the woman that gave birth to me.

"What's up, Mom?"

"Honey, can you bring me some Chapstick and ginger ale when you come by tonight? The dry lips are bad this time."

My shoulders slump, and I blow out a deep breath as tears prick my eyes. My mother's fighting her second round of breast cancer and is in the later stages of chemo. "Sure, Mom. Need anything else? I can run by the library if you need more books. I know I don't pick out the good romances. Sorry I'm not there."

"You have to work. You can't be here 24-7."

I cradle the phone between my ear and my shoulder while I type the Lorelei's Blissful Baked Goods information into my computer and immediately click on the *About Us* icon at the top of the page.

There she is. Lorelei Rogers.

What a beautiful name. Lorelei. I lip-sync it as my eyes scroll over each letter of her name on the screen. When I look up, Chase is squinting at me. "Uh, I'm looking up some stuff for Mom," I shrug, gesturing at the laptop screen. "I'm looking for…ginger ale."

"Try any grocery store, Liam."

"Are you there?" Mom asks through the phone. "Do you need me to let you go so you can catch bad guys?"

"Or girls," I mumble, scrolling back through Lorelei's website. I can't help but notice how professional the website is. It's colorful and tasteful. The road to hell is obviously paved with pink and the money to pay for website development.

"Have you caught a girl? Lordy, I'd love for you to catch a nice one. I was just reading this book about a woman who likes an older man. She doesn't seem like his type, but he does the dirtiest things to her. Smacking her bottom around with a brush like she did something really horrible. He calls it punishment, but I don't think she did anything wrong. I'm very confused."

Mom keeps explaining the book she's reading as I try to block out her daddy-dom book report and flip over to my case system to enter Lorelei's name, crossing my fingers she has a warrant out for her arrest for drug peddling or some other matter. Maybe I can use it to detain her and get her drug-pushing cart of depravity off the streets.

Nothing. She's clean as a whistle.

"Mom, I shouldn't hear this. Besides, there are no girls. You know me. I'm a dedicated bachelor and don't have time for a girlfriend."

"Sure, you do, sweetheart. I know you just go home and watch TV every night and make some popcorn. Unless you come over to see me, you're positively sad."

"Thanks, Mom."

"I'll let you go. Just don't forget the Chapstick. I'm about to rub Crisco on them or something."

"I'll remember, Mom."

"Such a good boy."

I hang up the handset and focus on the website in front of me. She even has a picture on the front page, and it's a nice picture. In my line of work, the pictures of drug dealers are mugshots. Lorelei Rogers blatantly flaunts her ability to sell marijuana out of her truck, and it's packaged as her in a pink dress with a white apron and holding a mix-breed puppy. When the fuck did selling drugs become like something out of a Hallmark movie? When did my job become chasing down a baker?

Fury fills my stomach. It happened with the legalization. Suddenly, marijuana is kittens and fucking glitter. I dedicated years to fighting marijuana use among teens, even teaching the S.T.A.R.T program to fifth graders for the past two years. As soon as it was legalized, every parent in the state had a party and toked up with their other suburban friends. Book clubs hit the bong. Knitting clubs passed the pipe. Every ounce of work done to prevent marijuana use over the last fifty years went up in smoke.

Literally.

Lorelei Rogers flaunts drugs in pretty brownies, and I will destroy her and send a message to anyone wanting to try similar bullshit shenanigans.

I scroll down and grab a block of sticky notes and a pen. Lorelei has a complete list of every concert and event she'll be at for the next month. Bingo. "I'm going to nail her," I say, spitting the pen cap on the desk and jotting down the heavy metal concert and country star tour dates.

"Yeah, you are," Chase says, fist-pumping the air. "Hit that hot drug dealer."

"I meant nail her legally. Not fuck her."

"Fuck the hot drug dealer. Fuck the hot drug dealer." He whisper chants and looks over his shoulder to make sure our coworkers aren't listening. It's not a good look for a drug task force agent to have carnal relations with a criminal.

I stand up and toss the rest of the sticky notes at him. He blocks the throw, and the sticky notes fall into his open coffee cup. "Dick," he says, grabbing a tissue to wipe the splash off his desk.

"That'll teach you." I push in my chair and turn to leave. At the last moment, I turn and swipe the cupcake into my trashcan as Chase sighs and looks longingly after it. "I'll see you later. I have to run errands for Mom."

"Sure, Lane. Errands."

I turn and face him. "What did you hear?"

He shrugs and looks back down. "I didn't hear anything," Chase says, going back to typing up a report for our latest surveillance on the meth dealer. "I sure didn't hear you tell your mom you'd go to the library and find her more daddy dungeon books to read."

Chapter 3

LORELEI

"Enjoy the concert," I say with a huge smile. There's no money for a weed truck quite like money from heavy metal concert-goers. "Thanks for your business. Take a business card."

The man with more piercings on his face than I can count grunts and clutches the paper bag of banana bread against his chest. Huh, I would have thought him a brownie guy, but maybe a nice slice of banana bread reminds him of his mother. Who am I to judge?

The line to my truck snakes around in a winding circle near the gate. Buddy Wilkens, already having eaten his free brownie, waves at me from the metal detectors at the concert entrance. His eyes droop, and he looks out of place at a metal concert in his usual overalls and short-sleeved shirt. It still amazes me that he's so amenable to having me here.

I wait on customers for twenty more minutes, then let Kailee take over when she comes into the truck, already sweating and looking tired from her sub job at the local high school. She puts her gloves and apron on, and I head back to the truck and put another pan of cookies into the oven. We're almost out. I should have known better with the type of concert.

Kailee and I have a flow down, and we work in tandem over the next half hour. The concert will start soon, and it'll be time to pack up. Until then, I flit around her, restocking the cases and setting the mixer for one more quick batch of cookies. I dump the green-colored butter into the batter and set the mixer to spin, the smell of the dough making my heart thump and my mouth water.

"Uh, Lorelei," Kailee mumbles. I turn to her and immediately freeze. Her brow is furrowed, and her usual smile is gone. She looks pale, and I instantly swipe the moneybox behind the oven. Kailee doesn't rattle easily, so something must be wrong.

"Just give him whatever he wants," I whisper, certain we're being robbed.

"Opposite problem. Officer McHottie is back." She jerks her head toward the window.

"McHottie?" a masculine voice scoffs at the front of the truck. "I'm here to talk to her. Tell her to step out of the truck."

I walk to the window, taking my apron off as I go. "Hi, Officer...I forgot your name." I didn't forget Officer Lane's name. I just don't want him to think that it's been on my mind since he snarled at me last week. I won't give him the satisfaction. He's here to make me feel small, and I'm going to beat him to it.

"Lane. Officer Lane," he says, flipping his badge out like I haven't seen it before. "Step out of the truck."

"I will when you tell me what this is about."

"Your permit is out of compliance."

I snort a little and cover my nose. "Officer Lane, my permit is six months old. It doesn't expire for another six months, and I assure you that it'll be renewed before the expiration date."

"No, Ms. Rogers." He smiles an evil grin.

"You found out my name. You must be a good detective," I say, leaning onto my elbows and propping my chin on my hands. I bat my eyes on purpose this time. "Amazing. Should I slow clap?"

"It's on your website. But your transportation permit should be within a foot of the window where customers can see it," he says, pointing.

I look at the permit in question. It sits at my right near the Square reader, the same position it was in the last time he was here. I silently point to it.

He opens a tape measure and puts the metal end of it against the window frame, stretching the tape measure to the framed permit as Kailee and I watch open-mouthed. "See, Ms. Rogers? One foot and a quarter inch. Clearly out of compliance. I need you to step out of the truck so I can write your ticket and give you the fine payment instruction," he says, releasing the tape measure with a clicking sound and a smirk.

Customers groan behind him and grumble something about donuts along with unflattering words about cops. Officer Lane ignores them. "You can't be serious," I deadpan.

"We can just move the permit closer," Kailee chimes in. "Here." She moves it a little to the right. "Measure again."

"I won't do that," he says, shaking his head.

"Why not?" I ask.

"I don't have to. You were out of compliance, and I'm fining you. One more fine, and I can take you to the station to process a bigger fine and make you appear in front of a judge to answer for why you're out of compliance. I can take you to the station now if you won't accept the fine."

I huff and grumble directions to Kailee. As soon as I head to the back of the truck, she's back to helping the customers like nothing's wrong. Fuck, I love her and her ability to sack up and keep going.

I open the back door to the truck like I'm ready to kick the door off the hinges. My nostrils flare as I jump down, but I immediately lament not dressing up for work today. Officer Lane strolls around, and my mouth opens without saying anything. I should have worn a sequined dress he couldn't take his eyes off of. Instead, I'm in faded jeans with holes at the knees, scuffed cowboy boots, and a simple off-the-shoulder t-shirt the same pink color as my truck. A hint of my white bra shows, and he squints at it.

He's taller than I thought. Maybe six and a half feet. His shoulders look wider when I'm below him. Not that I'm below him. Only looking up at him. But damn, I'd love to be below him and writhing in pleasure with my legs over those shoulders and biceps. I bet he's warm. Like a weighted blanket.

Even more surprising, his eyes are brown when he takes the aviators off. I make a "huh" sound and instantly bite my lip at his confused expression. I can't help but run my eyes the length of him. Strong legs. Strong arms. A perfect waist that probably has those gutter-like muscles on his sides above his groin. I can never remember what those are called, but they're the sexiest part of a man's body. I bet he'd moan my name if I licked him there.

Wait. What?

I clear my throat and blow out a breath. He puts his aviators back on, and I get the distinct feeling he does it only to check me out the way I'm checking him out. I should have grabbed my sunglasses before I left the truck so I could check him out and hide behind them.

He pulls out a ticket pad. "It's a fifty-dollar fine for the first offense. The second offense is a hundred dollars, but that's processed at the station. I'll take you in next time." He writes a few words on that pad, and I squint, standing on my tiptoes to see the ticket.

"Did you have this mostly filled out, Officer Lane?"

He pulls the pad up so I can't see it. "That's not your concern how I work."

"Because it looks like you already had my name and address filled in," I point to the top of the paper. "You just had to write in the offense. Is this entrapment? Did you come here looking for something specific or just whatever you could find?"

"That's not the way law enforcement works."

"You brought a tape measure."

"To make sure you were in compliance."

"Do you just carry tape measures around in your pants, Officer Lane?" I realize how it sounds as soon as the words leave my mouth. He stares at me, and I kick my boot below me, stirring up dust between us. He waves it away. "I meant to catch permit infractions. I didn't mean that you measure something else with them. I'm sure some guys do that, but I wasn't saying...You know what? I'll just shut the fuck up."

His face reddens. Did I embarrass him? Is he thinking about me measuring him with the tape measure? Because I totally am now.

"It's my job to make sure your licenses and permits are placed where they should be," he says in a husky voice.

I shake myself a little and square my shoulders. I need to get my shit together instead of drooling over a dickhead that's not here to flirt. "It's just interesting that Missouri has a serious meth problem, and you're here on a special mission to fine me for a paper being out of compliance a quarter of an inch."

His face reddens, and he flexes his jaw. All it does is make my panties wet. Fuck, he's gorgeous when irritated. "Are you resisting a fine?"

Why does his face look like he really wants me to resist? His chest heaves like he's trying to control panting of his own, and his hand flicks to his back pocket where he probably keeps his cuffs. His knuckles around the fine pad are white. Too bad I don't know if he wants me to resist the fine or resist him. He shifts his stance, and I don't look down, even though I have the sneaking suspicion that the crotch of his pants suddenly feels tight at the idea of me resisting him. That kind of guy, huh?

I can play along.

I arch my back and stick my C-cup tits out. I angle my face and reach up to twist my hair, letting it fall over my shoulder. He licks his lips before pointedly looking away from me. "I would never resist a big, strong man educating me on something I've done wrong. Where would a silly girl like me be without a man's correction? A man's guidance? Well, I'd be lost for sure. I'd drown in the danger of the real world," I drawl in my best Scarlett O'Hara voice.

His face reddens, and he nervously clicks his pen before looking at it like it just appeared in his hand. I move a few inches closer to him until I can smell his soap. Fuck, he uses woodsy soap. That's my weakness, and I need to be careful here or I'll drop to my knees and offer other ways to pay the fine.

"Stop being sarcastic, Ms. Rogers." He tears off the paper and hands it to me, careful to back up a few inches. "Pay your fine. If it's not paid in ten days, I'll be back."

I put my hands on my hips. "Why do I have a feeling you'll be back anyway?"

He turns and walks away without another word, shoving the ticket pad in his back pocket. He doesn't look back.

I look at the fine. Great. Fifty bucks I don't have. My business is booming, but the startup costs were high, and I'm just now breaking even and paying myself more than I pay Kailee. At least there's one good thing about the fine. His name is on the ticket.

Liam Lane.

I whisper his name, trying the words out as they roll over my tongue. Even his name makes my nipples hard, and my thighs reflexively rub together. It sounds like a superhero name or like he could be a dancer in *Magic Mike*.

He's an asshole, and I'm out fifty bucks for knowing him, but I like to watch him walk away.

Chapter 4

LIAM

"You did what?" I ask, slamming my hand on the desk between Chase and me. I grip the desk. If I don't, I'll punch the grin off his face.

"I ate it."

"It was in the trash."

"Yeah, but there was nothing else in the trash. It wasn't like there were used tissues or a stiff sock in there. It was still in the plastic case. I just pulled it out, took it home, and ate it after dinner. Slept like a fucking baby. You should try her stuff, man."

"I would never. We can't take drugs. We're the drug task force. What the fuck were you thinking?"

"I was thinking I wanted that cupcake the same legal way you went home and had a Bud Light."

"We haven't spent the last several years of our lives fighting Bud Light."

"Don't we always kind of fight Bud Light every time we pull over someone we think is drunk?" he asks, the grin still nailed onto his face.

I curl my lip. "We don't do that very often unless it's obvious. We aren't beat cops. We're the drug task force. We fight drugs. We don't swoon over their chocolatey goodness."

"Oh, it was fucking good. You should try it. Where did you say she parks? Because I have half a mind to go find this woman, pick her up in my arms, and take her to my man lair to make love to her. I'll keep her there, treating her like a princess forever, and let her bake all manner of things for me. I bet she's good at pie. Does she have pie?"

"I don't fucking know."

"I can imagine her rolling back and forth over the dough, her blond hair..." He trails off and looks at the wall behind me. "You said she was blond, right?"

"Strawberry blond," I grunt.

"I can see her rolling out that dough with her strawberry blond hair down." He stands in front of his desk, thrusts his hips like he's got a woman bent over the desk, and pretends he's rolling dough with a rolling pin. "The sun glistening off the crown of her head like she's a drug angel of the Lord."

"You're a foul human."

"When she's bad and adds too much cannabutter, I'll smack her rosy, little bottom like the naughty girl she is," he says, swatting the air and biting his lip. A female officer walks by and blushes, but he ignores her. "No jail for her. Only spankings with Daddy's bare hand. If she's blond, she probably has pale skin that'll show a red handprint on her ass, huh?"

I look down and will my burgeoning erection to go away at the thought of spanking Lorelei's ass. Not that I've seen her ass, but I've definitely imagined it. In the shower last night. In my bed this morning. I even got a boner while I was pushing the shopping cart around the grocery store and saw the bakery section.

I don't want to think about Chase's hand on her ass, though. Only my hand.

Fuck, this is a disaster. I shouldn't have gone back there. What was I trying to prove?

I'll also never admit that she was right. We have a huge meth issue, even in the suburbs, and I'm measuring her weed permit infractions when it's legal now. Logically, I know this, but I had to prove a point. All I ended up doing is fining a woman I really want to ask to dinner.

And fuck, I wanted to put my index finger out and pull up the fabric of her t-shirt over that bra strap so no other man could see it. The urge was so strong that I had to grip that fucking ticket pad or my hands would be all over her. Nothing like getting fired for using my position to assault a hot pot baker.

I put my head in my hands just as Chase walks off for another cup of coffee, laughing to himself. Why did I go back to her truck? What did I hope would happen? That she'd smile at me, and she'd be toothless? That she'd come out of the truck barefoot with feet riddled in bunions? Not that women with multiple bunions aren't worth a jerk-off session, but it would have helped the frequency to which I've touched myself to Lorelei since I saw her Friday night. My dick has a mild chafe, and I'm about ready to take a page out of my mother's book and dip into the Crisco.

Shit! I forgot to call Mom.

I hammer out her number on the work line, and it rings twice before she picks up. "How's my baby boy?" she coos. It doesn't matter that I'm thirty-three. My mother still thinks of me as four years old.

"Hi, Mom. How was your weekend since I saw you Saturday?"

"I'm feeling a little low."

"Nausea?"

She makes a humming sound. "It's much worse this time around. I hate complaining, though. How was your Saturday and Sunday?"

What do I say? That I went to a movie by myself on Sunday and did a couple drives by a house we're watching for work? That I went to Costco for a hotdog for dinner and thought about how nice it would be to have someone to take to a nice dinner or even cook for more than one person?

Mom talks to me about a recipe she's trying and invites me by for Friday after work, and I hang up after promising to replace her library books before I come over. I get through my workday, do my best to ignore the fuckface across the desk from me, and drive home under the speed limit. It's this thing I do when I have a bad day. I drive five miles under the speed limit and watch as everyone else slows down, not wanting to pass the cop. It gives me a tickle. Even though I don't have a beat cop cruiser, the black sedan with lights in the windshield looks official enough that people know they don't want to be pulled over by me.

I come into my apartment and sit on my Ikea couch with a sigh, cracking open a beer and not even bothering to turn on the TV or remove the badge in my belt. Mom's right. I'm fucking sad. My whole life is depressing.

I stand up and cross the room to my mantle to look at the pictures and ponder what they say about my life. A picture of Mom and me at a waterpark when I was fourteen sits front and center. No dad. No siblings. It was just us from the time Dad pulled the stereotypical walk out in the ruse of going to the store for milk. I run my finger over her face in the picture. I don't know what I'd do if I lost her. I don't have any other family except for some cousins I barely know scattered across the Southwest. The cancer came back, but the doctors say it looks good for remission.

If we can just get through the horrible chemo side effects, she'll be fine.

The other pictures are depressing. My old dog, Colonel, looks up at a younger me in a rusty frame I've had since I was a kid. He died right after I graduated from the academy, and starting a new career wasn't a good time to go to the shelter and get another dog. I close my eyes and remember what it felt like to run my hands through his Australian Shepherd mix fur. I blink away the water forming in my eye and move to the next photo.

A picture of me in a tux and my high school best friend, Amanda, going to prom always makes me smile. Tears fill my eyes for real now. She died from an overdose at her first college party. Maybe that's why I hate drugs so much. She only tried it one time. That's all it took. Some people can use for years and will be fine after a good colon cleanse and a week of fresh air at a Colorado rehab center.

Others aren't so lucky, and she was one of the unlucky ones.

It was cocaine. The rumor is that it had something else in it. Who knows? Everyone else at the party that shared the same lines was fine. Her family speculated there was an underlying heart issue she didn't know about. Whatever it was, she's gone, and I wish I could hug her again before strangling her for trying that shit.

Everyone leaves my life. Sure, I've dated a few girls, but none of them made me feel anything more than mild curiosity about their favorite foods. I've experienced lust and certainly take the edge off with an attractive woman when the opportunity presents itself, not even caring when they leave the next morning. But I've never met anyone that's taken my breath away and kicked me in the ass at the same time.

So, why can't I get a drug-pushing baker out of my damn mind?

It has to be simple lust. I've barely talked to her and only seen her twice. It's probably some scientific pheromone bullshit, like what Chase believes in.

I go back to the couch and stare at the wall, hating the silence in my head more than ever. Without stopping myself, I pull my ticket pad out of my side pocket and flip to Friday's ticket. Lorelei Rogers. I say it once under my breath. My finger traces her printed name, then finds her signature where I made her sign the triplicate form. Once I moon over the curly g in her signature, I slide my eyes to her address.

I found it in the system when I prepared her ticket. I always go into a situation prepared, and I knew I'd find an infraction. There are so many rules with growers and sellers now, and it's hard to walk the tightrope and follow them all. I knew damn well I'd get her on something, and I think about her address for the first time since I wrote it.

She lives on Caldwell Avenue and only a couple of miles from me. I know the neighborhood. Middle class. Low drug activity, which is the best any neighborhood could ask for. Even in upper-class neighborhoods, there's a heroin house.

I pull my phone out and tap her address into Google Maps. When I flip to the street view, a laugh bubbles in my chest. I'm not sure why I repress it. I'm alone and can't be judged like I would be at the precinct.

There she is. The Google car drove by to take the street view picture of a modest white bungalow with petunias lining the front sidewalk. Lorelei is out front by a black mailbox and making a thumbs-up motion and smiling as the car drives past, clearly posing for the street view picture. A dog, probably the same puppy on her website, sits dutifully at her feet and watches as the car passes. Looking closer, her dog looks like a mix. A lab mixed with rottweiler?

She adopts. She's not someone that wants a certain breed and pays hundreds of dollars for a dog. Her lawn is well-maintained. Then again, most drug dealers are functional and put on a show for their neighbors. Her hair is in a high ponytail in the picture, and the urge to reach into the picture and pull the elastic band out so I can see her hair fall over her shoulders hits me like a punch to the chest.

Before I can stop myself or question what I hope to glean from the outing, my hand is turning my doorknob and searching my pocket for car keys.

A simple drive by her house can't hurt, right?

Chapter 5

LORELEI

"Officer Tape Measure is here again," Kailee says, hands on hips. She blows a loose tendril of hair back, and I strain to hear the words over the band warming up inside the arena. "Want me to offer him a free cookie and a blow job, or should I pay him off from the cash register?"

"None of the above. That's bribing an officer, and he's too much of a stick in the ass to accept any, as tempting as blowing the fine officer may be."

I walk to the truck window where, sure enough, Officer Lane stands in a white work shirt and tie, looking out of place among the country concert crowd. Thankfully, we're just finishing up for the evening, and my eyes dart across the area to make sure we don't have an audience. Being hassled by the police would only improve my business and garner sympathy, but I don't like the stares.

I paste a smile on my face, and it's not entirely fake. Somewhere, mostly in my panties, I'm happy to see him again. Hopefully, it won't cost me in fines. "Hi, Officer Lane," I coo, tilting my head and winking. I do a funny shoulder shimmy and bite my lip. If he's going to harass me, he can deal with my sarcastic flirtation while he does it. "Cookie?" I ask, holding out a tray of wrapped and labeled chocolate fudge cookies.

"Step out of the vehicle."

I sigh and get out my own tape measure I put in the truck after the last run-in with him. "The sign is perfect now," I say, measuring from the window frame to the transportation permit and clicking the tape measure shut. "Eleven inches. Perfect size. Wouldn't you agree, Officer Lane? You really educated me last time. I love those eleven inches. Much more pleasant."

He clears his throat, and I wish I could read his eyes, but he has those damn aviators on again. "That's not the problem this time," he smirks, getting his own damn tape measure out and clicking the button. "Step out of the vehicle."

"Only if you tell me what this is about, Officer Lane."

"You're on public land."

"Bullshit. I'm on Buddy Wilken's patch of grass, and I have permission."

He crooks his finger in a come here motion, and I lean out the window to look where he points. "Missouri law is clear when it says private property only. Private property cannot include sidewalks, parking lots, or other walkways. Your wheel is half an inch on the walkway. Step out of the vehicle."

"You have to be fucking kidding me."

He rips his aviators off his face so fast that one of the arms nicks his nose, and he boyishly crinkles his eyes in annoyance. "Ms. Rogers, I asked you to step out of the vehicle. Am I going to need to come up there?"

"You need a warrant for that."

"Do you think I won't call in a request for one?"

"Once again, Officer Lane, the stupidity of worrying about my half an inch of wheel while meth dealers are currently buying forty packs of cough medicine and kitty litter at the local box store truly amazes me."

He walks to the back of the truck, and I lean out the window to see where he's going. It's only when he turns around to look at me again and his mouth drops open that I realize one of my boobs has fallen out of my t-shirt when I bent out the window. Sure, I have my bra on, but my loose V-neck t-shirt flops forward, showing the good officer my entire lace-covered tit.

He inhales sharply and closes his mouth as I try to stuff my boob back into my shirt. We're quiet for a moment as we stare each other down. "Open your back door for me," he finally says, his voice husky.

"Want me to open your back door for him, Lorelei?" Kailee snickers from the back of the truck. "I can pull it open for him real good." She bends forward and holds her stomach, squatting a little at the hilarity of juvenile back door jokes. Kailee has a history of peeing her pants when something is really funny. I don't really want a puddle right now, but the ass jokes are too much to turn down.

"No!" I say, jabbing my finger in the air. "If Officer Lane is going in my back door, he's going to have to force it open, and if he doesn't have permission to go in my back door, I'll have his back door."

"Good one," Kailee whispers from the floor.

The knob for the door rattles, and I stomp back to the window, leaning out and not caring that my boob falls out again. In fact, it feels nice like that in the warm breeze. "Officer Lane!" I yell.

His head appears from around back, only to duck behind the truck again. "Can you put your boob away, Ms. Rogers?"

"Does it bother you?"

"Open the door and step out."

"Not getting in my back door today, Officer Lane, and if you don't like my boob, don't make me lean out of the window and yell at you."

He steps from around the truck and flexes his jaw. "Are you gritting your teeth at me?" I taunt.

"No," he scoffs a little, and spit comes out of his mouth.

"Because you seem flustered." I move my shoulder a little so my boob sways below me. "Do you think I'm frustrating?"

Bingo. I can see him gulp from here, and he averts his eyes from my boob as he takes two deep breaths. He removes his phone from his black pants and presses a few buttons. "Yeah, this is Officer Lane, I'd like to call in a warrant."

"For fuck's sake," I grumble, taking off my apron, slamming it onto the counter, and stomping to the back of the truck.

"Don't do it," Kailee whispers, blocking the door. "He said he'd take you in next time."

I wrestle with her as she tries to block the door, her eyes wide, and her laughter from moments ago has turned to full-blown fear.

"It'll be better if I just get this over with instead of the swat team showing up for a half an inch of tire. You may get taken in too, and I need you to close up and drive home. I need you to just take the van home. Please, Kailee."

I push past her and open the door to find Officer Lane waiting, hands on hips. "No need for a warrant. See, I opened my back door for you."

He hangs up the phone, and I tilt my head, wondering if he was really calling in a warrant or some random fake number just to get me out of the truck. I fell for it. He smiles a little, like he thinks he got one up on me. "What's my fine?" I ask.

"Second offense is processed at the station," he says, turning me with his strong hands and pushing me up against the truck. The surprise of it shocks me, and my legs tremble.

Too bad I'm not sure if my legs are trembling because I'm in trouble with the police for the first time in my life or because Officer Lane's hands are traveling up my leg, checking me for weapons. "I'd like a female officer to do that," I say.

"Not something we allow unless a female is already present or there's a need for strip search."

"Do I need a strip search?" I ask, my voice trembling in fear for the first time. His hands stop over my jeans pockets, and my stomach roils with the knowledge he's bent behind me. His face is inches from my ass.

He clears his throat. "This will be enough. I don't think you're carrying weapons or drugs on your person. You're just selling poison from your death van."

"Fuck!" Kailee yells from the window. "Don't worry, Lorelei, I'm recording this," she says. Her phone is held in front of her. "He's manhandling a model citizen."

"Thanks, Kailee," I mumble as I shiver from Officer Lane's hands around my waist. Fuck, his hands are masculine and practically circle my waist as he places them on both sides of my waistband.

"Officer Half Inch won't get away with this!" Kailee yells from the window.

His hands stop moving. "Half inch?"

I snort, and he turns me around to put cuffs on me. Our eyes meet, and his chest stops moving for a few seconds as we stare at each other. His hands fumble with the cuffs, and I hum a little. He should be a pro at this, but he fumbles with my hands like it's his first time.

I need to break the silence. "You earned that nickname, Officer Half Inch. I'm afraid it's what I'll call you from now on."

He blows out a sigh and grits his teeth. "Let's go," he says, leading me to a black sedan parked nearby.

I look back at Kailee and thank the universe that she's still recording. Something tells me I'll want a copy of this for court...or posterity.

Chapter 6

LIAM

This is a dumb idea. Her scent fills the entire car. I've had some disgusting folks in my squad car, one man smelling so bad that I had to have the car detailed. I consider the same for Lorelei as soon as I get in and close the door, but for very different reasons. I don't know if I can *not* jerk off in my squad car if I don't get the body wash scent out.

I inhale deeply in the guise of breathing like I'm annoyed. Good. She'll think I'm irritated with her and definitely won't think I'm trying to identify what scent is wafting to the front of the car. It has a fruity smell but a little spice mixed in.

"Which station are we going to? I'll need to give Kailee the address so she can bail me out," she asks from the back seat. Her voice trembles, and a quick glance in the rearview mirror shows her lip trembling.

Fuck, I made her cry. I don't want her to sell drugs, but I didn't mean to make her cry.

I almost unbuckle my seatbelt and climb into the back seat so she can cry against my chest, getting my shirt wet with her tears, but I put the car into gear and straighten my face. I don't cuddle any other dealers that are upset in my car. Why would I cuddle her? "It'll take a long time to write the citation and process the paperwork. It's Friday night. You can call when you're ready to be picked up. You know you won't be put into general population, right? It's just procedure that I process you at the station and give you a higher fine. We're not taking your shoes and putting you in a cell. Just fingerprinting and mugshots. Nobody needs to bail you out, but you'll need a ride."

She sits back in her seat and looks out the window. The silence in the car, without her sassing me back and extolling the virtues of weed, is so unbearable that I clear my throat to keep from going crazy.

"Is Kailee the other woman at the truck? What's her story?" Fuck, I don't know why I'm talking. I can't help it. Must. Keep. Mouth. Shut.

She turns back to the front and scowls at me in the rearview mirror. "Do you actually care? Oh wait," she says, leaning forward. She puts her cuffs on the middle seat between us. I didn't put up the partition because she's not violent. It almost feels like an Uber ride. "You're going to look up Kailee as soon as we get to the station and write her up a fine, aren't you?"

"Why? She's trying to work and did a job. You're the owner and selling drugs out the back of your truck."

"I sell them from an attractive window with frosting and nuts added. Get it right."

"So, you admit that you sell drugs."

She cocks her head to the side and looks at me like I'm a moron. "Yeah, Dr. Watson. That's kind of the point. Drugs. Legal drugs that taste like heaven." She squints at the back of my neck. "Why do you hate me so much?"

I stomp on the brake so hard that Mom's library books in the front slide to the edge of the passenger seat, along with some entertainment magazines I checked out for her. I catch them with one hand before answering Lorelei. "I hate drugs, and I hate dealers. Thus, I have to hate you. I mean, I don't hate you on a personal level." I clear my throat. "You seem like an alright lady if I met you at the grocery store or something."

"The grocery store? Would you talk to me about the National Enquirer if we were in line together and I struck up a conversation about aliens?"

The realization I'd talk to her about aliens while holding laundry detergent and a gallon of milk creeps down my neck like an ice cube. Hell, I'd have a three-hour conversation with her about syphilis, complete with old-fashioned PowerPoint presentation, if that's what it took to talk to her.

This is bad.

I need to get this woman to the station, try not to get an erection when I touch her hand to guide her into the precinct, and never go back to the truck again. Maybe I'll call the health inspector I know from city hall happy hours and send him over to get Lorelei's drug den shut down. Maybe I should go after the food aspect instead of worrying about the drugs. A bad health inspection grade will shut it down faster.

Yeah, that's it. I'll just drop Lorelei off and never suffer this again. I'll go to a bar, drink until the bartender looks good, and take her home for a fun night. I'll squeeze my eyes shut when I pass pink trucks and never go into a perfume section of a store or look at a rottweiler mix again.

"I didn't figure you for a daddy dom guy."

I almost hit the brakes again, and we both lean to the side as the car swerves. "Excuse me?" Did she just ask if I was dominant sexually? It takes a few seconds to right the car as I think about what she'd feel like squirming under me.

"Did you just almost get in an accident because I asked about your books?" she shrieks from the back seat. "Jesus fucking Christ!"

The fucking books. I look in the mirror and notice she's staring at them in the front seat. "I didn't almost get in an accident. There was a squirrel in the road."

"There was no squirrel."

I bang on the steering wheel. "There was a fucking squirrel. Right back there!" I yell, jabbing my finger over my shoulder.

"There wasn't a squirrel, Liam," she deadpans in a calm voice.

Silence fills the space between us. My heart speeds up, and my stomach feels like I'm in a falling elevator. "How do you know my first name?"

"It was on the first fine you gave me. I'm a good citizen and read my paperwork, Liam Lane." She smiles, and my pants feel tight. Even if the smile is sarcastic and a blatant attempt to get one up on me, I can't help but admire it and revel in the fact that I made her smile.

She sits back again, and the sound of my car leather squeaking as she moves away from me makes my teeth grind. "They aren't my books. They're my mother's."

"Sure, Liam," she laughs. "Blame your mommy for your car smut."

I blow out a real sigh this time. "She has cancer and doesn't feel the best after the chemo treatments. I run errands for her until she feels better. She asked me to return books and get her more and a few magazines. I went to the library on my lunch today and picked some out I thought she'd like." I run my hand through my hair, and the back of my neck reddens like the skin there knows she's staring at it. "I don't know why I'm explaining any of this to a drug dealer."

I look in the mirror and see her brow furrowed. Before she can say anything sassy back to me, my phone rings, and I grab it. Lorelei laughs as soon as I press the green button and grumbles something like, "So much for hands free laws when it's a cop, huh?"

I ignore her and answer. "Yeah, Mom."

"Hi, baby," Mom says through the phone. "Did you forget to bring my books by? I made your favorite chicken and noodles with garlic bread."

"Shit! I'm sorry Mom. I didn't forget. I just got busy with something else."

As soon as the words are out of my mouth, my phone pings in my hand. I pull over and look at it quickly while Mom talks about what she made for dinner and how she has nothing to read while holed up on the couch tonight. I open the text message from Chase and curse.

"Why are you cussing, Liam?"

"Sorry, Mom. Chase texted and said there was a bar brawl, and the station is packed with bookings. I have a perp in my car and can't get her booked right now. I was hoping to come over, but I'll probably have to wait with her."

Tapping on my shoulder startles me, and I jump, almost dropping the phone. "Just take the books to your mom. We can swing by," Lorelei says with a shrug.

I look at her like she's crazy, my mouth open and my nose crinkled. "What the fuck is wrong with you? I'm taking you in for a fine process, and you want me to run an errand to my mom? I don't want criminals to know where she lives."

"Why not? I'll stay in the car."

"What the fuck do you mean? Do you want drug dealers knowing where *your* mother lives?"

She looks at me and cocks her head to the side. "So we're just going to sit out front of the station while your mother needs books and cooked dinner for you."

"Damn right."

"Liam, sweetheart, are you there?"

"Yeah, Mom," I say, holding the phone back up to my ear. "I was talking to the woman in my car."

"Oh, a woman! You have a woman in your car. Is it a date? You sure could use a date. When was the last time you had one?"

Lorelei blows out a laugh next to me, and I turn the volume down on my phone. She hears every word, and I put my finger in the air, telling her it'll be a minute.

"Mom, I have to take her in. I'm booking her."

"Kinky. She must have done something really naughty for you. Good for you, dear."

Lorelei falls into the seat behind her and covers her mouth with laughter as I turn the volume down on the phone so I can barely hear my mother. "It's not like your books, Mom. I'm arresting her."

"What'd she do?"

"Sold marijuana-laced brownies out of a truck. She's a wretched person, Mom," I growl, looking at Lorelei in the back seat as she holds her stomach and silently laughs. Great.

"Isn't that legal now?" Mom asks.

"Thank you, Mrs. Lane!" Lorelei yells from the backseat. "Tell your son."

I put the phone in my lap and turn to face Lorelei. "How can you still hear her?"

"I have excellent hearing. It's the brownies."

My stomach growls as soon as the words leave her mouth. Not that I want Lorelei's brownies, but I desperately love my mother's chicken and noodles with garlic bread.

As if reading my mind through the phone, my mother sighs. "I also made green beans with bacon fat."

"Mom," I groan. "I'm so hungry. This isn't helping."

Lorelei leans forward and taps me on the shoulder again. I put the phone down and turn back to her. She's dangerously close, and if it was any other drug dealer in my car, I'd take evasive action. Since it's her, it's all I can do not to push my lips forward a few inches and see if her lip gloss tastes as good as it looks. My tongue darts out of my mouth to lick my lips, and her eyes flick to my mouth. "Just stop at your mom's. She needs her books, and you need food. I can wait in the car. She sounds nice. I'd never hurt an innocent old woman."

"I'm not leaving you in the car. It's ninety degrees outside," I mumble.

"Leave the car on."

"You could steal it."

"Crack the windows like I'm a dog."

"Liam? Are you coming or not? I need to know if I have to put this in Tupperware," Mom's voice says from somewhere near my leg.

I put the phone back to my ear, still staring at Lorelei. I can't take my eyes off her. "Mom, that won't work. I can't leave the perp in the car."

Lorelei sits back and huffs. "Well, dear, you can bring your little friend."

"She's not a friend, Mom," I grunt, pinching my nose and squeezing my eyes shut in irritation.

"Then, why do you sound so friendly with each other?"

"We're not, Mom. She's a drug dealer."

"For pot brownies? She's not a drug dealer. Just bring your friend over. I have to get the garlic bread out of the oven. Luckily, I made enough. You bring that young lady over," she says in a stern tone she doesn't usually take with me before hanging up the phone.

I stare at the phone for a few seconds like I can't believe my mother told me to bring a drug bust over to her house for dinner. "This isn't happening," I whisper under my breath.

"Oh, it's totally happening. I'm hungry. Let's go to your mom's house." Lorelei claps her hands like this is all good fun.

I turn my head to face her again. "How are you hearing that?"

"I told you, Officer Half Inch. It's the brownies. It gives me mutant hearing." She smiles and leans back against my back seat. This isn't good. I can't have a woman smiling at me like that and take her home to meet my mother.

"Fine, but you stay cuffed. I don't need you trying to run off and break into a random garage to hacksaw your cuffs off."

"I find it funny that you think my life is like the plot of *The Fugitive*."

"Criminals are criminals, Ms. Rogers," I say, pulling back into traffic and turning toward my mother's house.

Chapter 7

LIAM

"Hi, Mom!" I yell and walk into the house, the smell of garlic bread making my mouth water as soon as the screen door squeaks shut behind me.

Well, behind Lorelei. She stands behind me, her cuffs still around her wrists, nodding around the house like she gets a say in whether or not she approves of my mother's home. I look around and take in the house with fresh eyes, wondering what she sees.

The TV I mounted on the wall last year shows an old sitcom from thirty years ago. The coffee table contains a neat stack of books ready for me to return to the library, and I walk over to swap them for the books under my arm. Empty mugs with used teabags litter the coffee table and end table, and an afghan is bunched on the couch. Tissues and popsicle sticks litter the floor.

"Mom?" I ask again, nudging Lorelei into the room further and walking her to the couch. I look at Lorelei as she eyes the titles of Mom's daddy romance books. "Stay here," I instruct, pointing my finger in her face. Her eyes cross as she stares at my fingertip a centimeter from her nose.

"Aren't you going to take the cuffs off?" she asks.

"No. This isn't exactly routine. You're only here because the station is experiencing an overwhelming booking issue, and you're annoying enough to nag me to bring you along."

"I'm not annoying. You wanted to bring me. Wittle Wiam's tummy is rumbly."

"Is this your lady friend?" Mom asks, shuffling into the room and saving me from admitting to myself that I want to hang out with Lorelei a little longer.

Mom looks old in her bandana that covers her head and hangs over her shoulder. Her eyes have dark bags under them, and she shuffles like a woman older than her sixty years. She looks eighty with new wrinkles forming around her mouth.

"Mom, this is Lorelei. She belongs in jail."

Mom looks at Lorelei for a moment, her eyes moving over Lorelei's face and hair. She tilts her head to the side as if looking at a new appliance she's considering buying. "Aren't you beautiful? Orange wouldn't be your color at all, but you'd be perfect for my Liam. I'm Nola."

"It's nice to meet you, Nola. I don't belong in jail, and your food smells delicious. You must be quite the cook."

Mom blushes. "Oh, I just dabble."

"I've always wanted to cook savory meals. I'm a baker. Cooking and baking are two separate skills. Wouldn't you agree?" Lorelei asks, smiling. Why is she smiling that gorgeous smile at my mom?

"Well, between the two of us, we could keep my dear boy fed, huh?" Mom giggles.

I need to stop this matchmaking, smiling, and giggling now.

"Mom, let me help you with this stuff," I say, bending down to pick up the popsicle sticks and tissues and shoving them in the used mugs. I grab a few items and head to the kitchen, hurrying back because I don't want Lorelei to attack my mother. I don't think she would hurt an old woman, but drug dealers are deceiving. Flashes of my mother being choked out by Lorelei's handcuffs and held hostage as Lorelei backs out of the house and runs away enters my mind.

"Thank you," Mom says in a weak voice. She shuffles back to the kitchen. "Such a dear boy."

"What are you doing? What do you need? I can get it, Mom. Go sit down."

She shoos me off. "Nonsense. I'm getting my second wind for the day." She nods back to the room. "Who's your lady?"

"She's not my lady. She runs a cannabutter baked goods truck that's in violation of permit law." I yell the last part so Lorelei will hear me from the living room.

"I am not, Mrs. Lane. Your son has a stick about half an inch up his butt."

Mom giggles and pushes me out of the kitchen. "She's pretty," she whispers. "Go in there and talk to her. Tell her about your superhero figure collection and your eczema in the winter. Better to come clean now."

"I don't want to talk to her, Mom. She's not a date. She's a person I'm taking to the station, and I sure as hell don't want to talk to her about my skin condition from dry air."

"Uh huh."

I trudge into the living room, plop down across from Lorelei, and frantically think of something to take the focus off her and how perfect we'd be for each other. "I'll take your books back, Mom," I yell.

"Thank you, dear," she calls, still puttering around the kitchen.

I look at Lorelei and flick my gaze away. She must know I'm uncomfortable because she stares at me. It's a forced stare. I can tell she doesn't want to look at me any more than I want to look at her when she's settled into my mom's couch like a tick. Like she belongs there.

With nothing else to do, I grab one of the entertainment magazines off the top of the library book stack as Mom walks back into the room and circles the coffee table to take a seat right next to Lorelei. I flick through the magazine and try to find something to change the subject. Anything. "Oh look, an interview with Eminem."

"Was it the green one or the red one?" Mom asks, fluffing the pillow behind her and placing a bowl of cashews and two mini cans of Coke on the coffee table. My mother smiles at Lorelei, and my heart drops. I know that look. Mom likes her. "Personally, I like the yellow peanut one. He always has the goofiest voice in those Santa commercials. What do you think?"

Lorelei opens her can of Coke and takes a sip of foam off the top, slurping so loud that my dick notices. "I like whatever color the plain guys are. The round costumes make me laugh. And those gloves are ridiculous."

I put my head in my hands. This isn't happening. A drug dealer on the way to fingerprinting isn't in my mother's living room talking about candy commercial costumes confused with rapper interviews while casually drinking a soda. It can't possibly get any worse.

"What smells so good besides the garlic bread, Mrs. Lane? I smell something vegetable-like."

"Oh, sweetie, I made Liam's favorite meal."

Lorelei smiles at my mom like they're best friends. "What exactly is Liam Lane's favorite meal?" At least she didn't call me Officer Half Inch to my mom.

"Chicken and noodles, green beans, and garlic bread. Would you like some? I have plenty."

"I'd love some, ma'am. I worked up an appetite with your son manhandling me and putting me in cuffs."

Mom pushes off the couch again, and I jump up. "Mom, sit down," I gently push her back down to the couch. "You've done enough, and you'll wear yourself out. Let me get my plate and yours."

"And Lorelei's."

I groan and pat her on the shoulder. "Fine. Fine. I'll get the drug dealer I'm taking in for a fine a plate of food."

Lorelei and Mom chat about books as I stomp to the kitchen a little harder than necessary, my boots hitting the linoleum so hard that I worry I'll crack the flooring. I scoop the food onto plates as my mouth waters from desperation. I'm going to make sure Mom has food first. If Lorelei thinks she's getting first plate, I have news for her. I scoop extra green beans onto Lorelei's plate, rattling the spoon a little louder than necessary to drown out Mom and Lorelei's conversation about romance books they've both read.

I clear my throat loudly before walking in and placing a plate in front of Mom with a smile and a plate in front of Lorelei with an exasperated sigh.

Lorelei's shoulders bunch up, and she smiles, clapping her hands as much as the cuffs allow. I go back to the kitchen and bring out my own plate, pulling the recliner over so I can use the coffee table as a table. I dig into my food and don't hide my eyes fluttering as I bite through Mom's noodles. I rotate between each dish, and I frequently steal glances at Lorelei as she chews. If her facial expression is any indication, she likes Mom's cooking.

Mom will talk about this for years. That nice girl I brought to her house in cuffs that ate every scrap of food on her plate and talked to her about M&M commercials and BDSM books.

"Was Liam Lane always so uptight?" Lorelei asks.

"Fuck," I mumble under my breath.

"Always," Mom says, scooping green beans into her mouth with a shaky hand. I want to go over and help her eat, but I'd get swatted if I did something like that for her. "Had a stick up his rear since first grade."

"That's not true. I'm fun."

"When was the last time you did something fun?" Mom asks, her fork halfway to her mouth like I stumped her.

"Whose side are you on?"

"Yours, honey, but you need a little fun in your life. You don't go to concerts. You don't go to movies or hike on weekends. You only go out for beer with the guys from work, and most of them have sticks further up their butt than yours. Except for that handsome partner, that is. Otherwise, you mope around the house."

"Am I supposed to just be loose and lawless like Ms. Rogers here? What do you want? Am I supposed to go to a Tijuana donkey show every weekend and snort lines of cocaine out of a hooker's butt crack?"

"It would make you more interesting, dear," Mom says. "But what's a donkey show?"

"Never mind, Mom."

Lorelei sips her Coke and looks over at me, batting those damn eyelashes. I give her a stern look, warning her not to talk. "Why don't you explain it, Liam? Tell your mother what a donkey show is."

"I will not."

"Then why'd you bring it up?"

"Don't argue, you two. I'll look it up on the internet later. But to answer your question, Lorelei, Liam was uptight even before Amanda."

My stomach roils, and I stare at my plate. "I don't want to talk about Amanda."

"Is Amanda your ex or something? Did she break Liam Lane's cold heart, rendering him incapable of empathy?" Lorelei asks, clutching her chest and smiling.

Silence fills the room. "Amanda's dead," I mumble. I shove another piece of garlic bread into my mouth and stare out the window while I chew, focusing on not meeting either woman's eyes.

Out of the corner of my eye, I see Lorelei swallow and look down at her own plate. "I'm sorry. I didn't know," she whispers. "I just thought she dumped you."

"Oh, nothing like that," Mom says, waving her hands, clueless to my unease at the conversation. She's always been that way a little. Mom's a sweet lady, but she's a little naïve and can go off on a tangent if she wants to talk about something, oblivious to the fact that other people don't want to talk about a topic. "She was Liam's best friend in high school and died of an overdose at a college party."

Tears well up in my eyes, and I focus on eating. I will not cry in front of a bust. I take deep breaths through my nose and try to control my chest from moving with the movement. I can control this.

"Is that why you hate drugs so much?"

My eyes flick to Lorelei's face, and her face shows nothing but sympathy. Her cheeks are pink, and her eyes are kind. "Among other reasons."

"Being?"

I drop my fork, and it startles my mother. She jumps a little, and I reach out and pat her shoulder in apology. "I've seen a lot of kids get sucked into drugs. They started by sneaking their parents' weed in middle school. By high school it was harder stuff."

Lorelei looks down and begins eating again. I shovel the last of the noodles into my mouth, but they're now tasteless. Now I'm thinking about Amanda and how I probably haven't done something truly joy-inspiring for ten years.

"Well, when are you two going on a date?" Mom asks, and I cough food out of my nose.

"Oh, Mrs. Lane, I would never be good enough to date Liam. With me being a drug dealer and all," Lorelei says. "And I don't like donkey shows."

"We're not dating, Mom."

Mom shuts her mouth and looks...sad. Does she really want me to date a woman with a weed food truck?

"But I do need you to take me somewhere, Liam Lane," Lorelei says.

"I'm taking you to booking after dinner. They're probably clearing the bar brawl out." I check my phone and fire off a text to Chase, asking him if it's safe to bring her in.

"I need to check on Bogey."

"Who or what is Bogey?"

"My dog. I just want to run by my house and check on him. Kailee's probably still closing and going home, and he has to pee. Poor thing won't last me spending hours getting booked. If he poops in his kennel, he eats it. You don't want my dog to have to eat his own feces because you're wasting my time over half an inch, do you?"

"You want me to drive you to your house so you can let your dog out?"

"I don't have a fence. We need to walk him."

My face burns, and I run my hand through my hair. "I'm going to get in trouble for this."

"I won't tell anyone that your mother made me dinner and you stopped so we could walk the dog. It's not like I'm running guns or something. In fact, I'm of the opinion you'll get in trouble for bringing me in on a busy Friday night for something so stupid anyway."

"Liam, you heard the lady," Mom says, standing and taking my dish. "You can't have the dog eating its own crap."

Chapter 8

LORELEI

"I can't believe I allowed this," Liam grumbles.

"I thought it was just signing a few fines and having my picture taken? It's not like I robbed a bank." He stands behind me while I fumble with my house keys, trying to unlock my door while still in cuffs. "If you'd take the fancy bracelets off, I'd be able to do this faster, Officer Half Inch."

"Back to Officer Half Inch?" he asks.

I look over my shoulder and smile the grin that I've used on other men. Liam's face flushes, and his lips part like inhaling through his nose isn't enough to take proper breath. "I wanted to impress your mother. She's nice. It's hard to believe that you came out of her vagina."

He makes a gagging motion and looks away. "Can we not talk about my mother's vagina?"

"Sure," I say. The key finally gives in the lock, and I open the door to the familiar smell of my house.

I inhale, enjoying the scent of the fudge I made earlier today and the vanilla candles and incense I use often. The combination makes my house smell like a candy store, and I smile at the thought of my own Willy Wonka house.

I smile now, even if I'm wearing handcuffs.

"I'll just let Bogey out of his kennel. It's in the laundry room. Do you need to escort me? You can't have me bolting out the back door."

Liam looks around my small bungalow like he's never been in a woman's house before. His neck cranes to the side, trying to look at the other rooms, and he walks over to my living room bookshelves to peruse the titles. "You like to read romance, too," he mumbles. "What is it with the filthy romance and women?"

"We like happy endings and strong men that fight for their women. What's wrong with that?"

"Huh, I took you for a feminist."

I frown and squint, blowing a bit of hair out of my face with a huff. "Actually, a lot of the women are strong characters and enjoy sex on their terms. Sure, there are some that aren't, but I don't read those. Why do you have to yuck my yum?"

"Yuck your yum?" He looks back to the shelf. "You're into vampires and werewolves, huh?"

A yip from the laundry room interrupts the words on the tip of my tongue, and I head to the back of the house to free my best friend from his kennel. I feel Liam behind me, but he doesn't keep up. Is he looking around my house as he walks through it, taking in my light-colored furniture and pastel walls in robin egg blue or butter yellow? Is he comparing it to his place? Part of me wonders if he has all black furniture and gray walls with black curtains on the windows. I bet his house looks like a jail cell.

Bogey wags his tail as soon as I open the door to the laundry room. His brown eyes light up, and he yips and paws at the kennel as I unlock the cage.

"Why do you put him in a kennel when you leave?"

"I only kennel him if I'll be gone more than a few hours. He has separation anxiety," I say, bending down and kissing Bogey's nose. He licks my cheek, and I giggle. Even though I'm being taken to jail in a few minutes, Bogey always cheers me up. "The vet said his kennel feels like a safe place for him. If I leave him out for too long, he eats through the drywall, probably trying to escape the house to come after me."

Liam approaches right behind me, and Bogey locks eyes with him. My dog instantly wags his tail like he does to all guests, and Liam strokes his head. "Do you like dogs?" I ask.

"Love them," he says sadly.

"Did you have one as a kid?"

"As a teen," Liam says, bending next to me. I catch another whiff of the soap smell I smelled the first time we met. The urge to bury my face in his neck and inhale is powerful, and I shake my head, remembering he's a cop and taking me in for mugshots.

"What happened?" I ask. I should keep my mouth shut, especially after that Amanda fuck up at dinner, but I can't help myself.

"My mom let me have one if I promised to take care of him." Liam ruffles Bogey's fur, and there's a hint of smile on the cop's face for the first time since he fake smiled at me the first time he harassed me. It's nice to see him somewhat happy. "I took care of him until he died right after I got out of the academy. It wasn't the time to get a new dog, much less a puppy."

"I think my dog likes you, but I need to get him outside so he doesn't excitement piss on the floor."

Liam stands, and I fumble to push myself up with only my thighs. I'd usually push off the floor with my hands, but getting up from the floor in handcuffs isn't as easy I thought it'd be. I roll onto my left thigh and try to heave myself up. Before I can push off the floor, Liam steps closer to me.

I'm still on the floor, and his knees are in front of my face. I look up into those damn brown eyes, and he puts his hand on my arm. "Let me help you," he says, pulling me up.

His hand is warm on my skin. Burning, really, and my breath leaves my lungs. His hand is only on my arm. What would it feel like on my breasts or sliding up my legs? Why am I even thinking that? This is a jerk that's taking me to the police station for permit violation paperwork.

Trembling, I get my legs under me and get off the floor as Bogey yips and runs to his leash on the wall hook near the back door. "Um," I say, trying to find the words. My voice trembles, and I clear my throat to get myself together. "Can you walk him while I watch from the porch? I don't want my neighbors to see the cuffs and think I'm a bad person if they're on their back porch or looking out the window."

Liam tilts his head and scowls. "They don't know you run drugs?"

"Run drugs? Those are strong words. I make baked goods with legal ingredients. If I go out in these cuffs, they'll either think I robbed a Target or that we're into some kinky shit since you'll be with me. They'll probably shake their heads and cluck something like, 'I knew that Rogers girl was into some *Fifty Shades* shit.'" I hold up the cuffs and widen my eyes.

He blushes and runs one of his delicious, masculine hands up the back of his neck. "Are you into *Fifty Shades* stuff? I saw the *Fifty Shades of Grey* series on your shelf."

We stare at each other for seconds, and the only sound in the room is Bogey's paws against the wall as he tries to get his leash. I shake my head a little like I'm shaking cobwebs from my ears. "Did you just ask if I'm into BDSM?"

Liam blushes, and it surprises me. Who knew he could be embarrassed? I thought him devoid of actual human emotions. "I'm sorry," he mumbles. "I don't know where that came from."

"What the fuck, Liam?"

He pinches his nose and looks down, and I walk away, heading to the door and clipping Bogey's leash on him. When I turn back around, Liam's at my side, his eyes only on Bogey. "Do I need poop bags?" he asks, obviously trying to change the subject. It's on the tip of my tongue to fuck with him and tell him I really do like to be spanked, but I don't know what that would do to him, and I'm mildly afraid of what it could lead to.

I grab a roll of compostable poop bags from the shelf above my head and hand them to Liam. He takes them, his fingers touching mine again, and he opens the door as I try to ignore the fluttering in my stomach.

I head out behind him and stand on my small back deck. Liam looks around as Bogey circles his feet. "What the absolute fuck?" He stares at my makeshift greenhouse made of PVC and clear plastic on the deck. It's the size of an old outhouse and full of marijuana plants. Liam's mouth drops open, and he blinks about five times before he gasps like he just found a money laundering ring in my basement. "Are you kidding me?"

"Do you want to see my grower permit?" I ask, completely calm since I know that I'm in perfect compliance here. "Where did you think I get my goods?"

He stares at the greenhouse and then looks back to me. He looks between the greenhouse and me a few more times like he's watching a rousing game of ping pong. "Want me to unzip so you can look? It's a pretty sweet setup, and I make sure that I don't use any pesticides or any other chemicals. All of my baked goods are one hundred percent organic."

I straighten my shoulders and stand up straight. I'm proud of how I run my business, growing my own plants and infusing the cannabutter in my own kitchen. I've even had the health inspector at my house and in the food truck. I keep my nose clean, and I love rubbing it into Liam's face. The look on his face is priceless, and I wish I could take a picture. He looks positively nauseated.

Bogey pulls on the leash, and Liam tears his eyes away from the greenhouse long enough for my dog to lead him to a patch of grass and unload a torrent of pee on the nearby oak tree. Liam bends down to pat Bogey and whisper something to my dog. I strain my ears, but I can't hear what he says. Probably something like, "Good dog."

"Do you want to see my kitchen while you're here?" I ask. I'm pretty proud of my kitchen, but I'm also stalling. I'm not looking forward to a police station visit. "You can see that my place is clean so you won't send the health inspector out."

Bogey squats in a poop position, and Liam flicks his eyes away from my dog to give the animal privacy. "Sure. You've had dinner with my mother, and I've taken your dog to the bathroom. May as well make a night of this."

Liam takes care of Bogey's poop with the bag I gave him, and I point to the bins at the side of the house. As soon as Liam's back, I pick up Bogey, give him a kiss, and wave Liam into the house. "You can wash your hands in the bathroom if you want," I say, waving in the direction of my bathroom and walking to the kitchen, Bogey yipping at my heels. "I need to give Bogey his treat."

As I rummage through the treat bag, pat Bogey, and tell him he's a good boy, I hear the water run in the bathroom as Liam mutters something to himself about a lot of pink in the bathroom. He's probably referring to my homemade soap and my pink hand towels neatly stacked on the farmhouse sink.

When he walks back into the room, I wave my hands like I'm Vanna White on *Wheel of Fortune*. Well, as much as I can in cuffs. "Welcome to where the magic happens."

Liam's eyes dart around my kitchen that's decorated in the matching colors of my food truck, my industrial fridge, my three white mixers on the counter, and my stools under the snack bar. "Want a cup of tea?" I ask, pointing to the stools.

He shrugs. "Why not? You won't put weed in it, will you? No poison?"

"Nope. It's simple green tea," I explain, turning and grabbing the kettle from the stove. "Are you this accommodating to everyone you bring in?"

"Absolutely not."

I laugh a little and put the full kettle on the stove before turning on the burner and getting the mugs from the nearby cabinet. "Why are you allowing it now?"

"I'm interested in what makes you tick." The words shock me, and I spin around so fast some of my hair slaps my cheek. He's interested in me? "If I know how you work and what motivates you, maybe I can get you to stop this and become a model citizen."

"I am a model citizen."

"Right," he scoffs.

"What makes you tick?" I ask. "Amanda's death?"

"Maybe a little. I've already told you, though. How did you start doing this?"

I lean over the counter, and my V-neck opens a little again. I don't hide it. He's in my house, and he's already seen my bra. His eyes move to my cleavage, and he licks his lips. Good to know the fine officer is a breast man. "Are you asking for my villain origin story, Officer Lane?" I ask, my voice husky.

"Yes, Ms. Rogers." His eyes move to mine again, and they're dilated into dark, wide holes. I wonder if mine are the same for him. It's been a long time since I've had a handsome man in my home or in my bed, and his bedroom eyes make my stomach queasy. "I want to know all about…" His voice trails off, and his chest moves up and down. He grips the counter, and the whites of his knuckles show again. "I want to know all about how you chose this for yourself."

Chapter 9

LIAM

I'm going to have to come four hundred times and jerk my dick clean off to get this woman and her cleavage out of my mind. What the fuck is wrong with me, and why am I looking at her cleavage like they're twin mounds of mashed potatoes I'd like to butter and stick my face into?

The fact that this woman is so perfect, so damn loveable, and even has a sweet dog that I'd steal if I got a chance is maddening. I don't know whether to turn her over my knee and spank her for her misbehavior or gently kiss my way from her feet to her ears while I make her come on my fingers.

The thought of both runs through my mind.

I'm so utterly destroyed by everything in this woman's house. The scent of candy. The pink of her bathroom and her kitchen, even though I've never been able to stomach the color until now. Damn her and her ability to get away with selling drugs and even making pink attractive. If I could find a way to legally burn her greenhouse crop,

I'd pick her up, carry her to her bedroom, and slide my dick in and out of her until she screams that she'll behave for the rest of her life.

"I've always been a great baker," she says proudly, and I crinkle my eyes, momentarily forgetting that I asked her a question. I'm still thinking about spanking her. Her head is tilted, and loose hair is spilling down her cheeks. It's all I can do not to push it behind her ear.

"Why do I see you with a baked good stand as a little girl? You used to sell lemonade with cookies and brownies, right?"

"How did you know?"

"I'm a cop. I have an eye for these things. You seem like the lemonade stand type, even now."

The kettle shrieks, and she turns to get it off the stove and pour the hot water into two mugs with tea bags. I take the time to check out her ass while she does it.

As far as asses go, it's damn near perfect. Rounded at the back but rounded up, not out. Her waist is thin, and her legs are long and lean, perfect for wrapping around my waist while I...

"Do you take anything with your tea?"

I clear my throat and set my face into what I call my cop expression. A grim line. "A little sugar."

She adds sugar from an almost empty sugar bowl and puts the cup in front of me. "Anyway, I got into health stuff," she says, pulling out a stool and sitting next to me like we're good friends having a chat.

Damn, I want to be friends with this woman. Really good friends. The urge hits me like a board to the face.

"I was what you'd probably call granola," she says, and I force my mind to focus on what she's saying and not what I'd like to do to her.

"I'd still call you granola."

She smiles. "I got into natural herbs, tinctures, and essential oils. But the one thing I couldn't stop was baked goods. I love pie and would never give it up. Do you like pie?"

"I enjoy a good pie on occasion."

Fuck, I sound like an idiot, but I like pie. I also wouldn't mind eating *her* pie, and I don't mean the kind stuffed with fruit. In fact, if she weren't a common drug pusher I'm taking in for processing, I'd spend my Friday night spreading her legs on the kitchen counter and burying my face in her pussy. My mouth waters at the thought. What would she taste like? Sugar, spice, and everything nice?

"I finally decided not to fight my love of baked goods and combine my two loves. Holistic living and good pastry. And here we are," she says, waving her handcuffed hands around her kitchen. "I got a food truck because food trucks are hot, applied for all the permits when marijuana became legal, and an officer of the law is now in my kitchen harassing me for making people happy."

"You make people high."

"Right. Happy."

We slurp our tea in silence as I look around her kitchen. She said the health inspector has already been out, but I catalog little things I can point him to. A small hole in the floor the size of a penny that a mouse could get through if it wanted. The temperature setting on the fridge. Could I bump it up a couple of degrees without her looking before we leave? Does she sanitize the dishes she uses to bake her death wares? I don't see sanitizer, but it could be under the sink. She keeps her counters clean.

Before long, my cup is empty, and I slide off my stool, adjusting myself a bit to cover the burgeoning erection for this woman. Sanitation inspections aside, I can't get the idea of taking her for my own out of my mind.

Mine.

Is that what I want? Why her? Of all the women I've met that go to church and work as kindergarten teachers and librarians, why is the drug-dealing baker the only one that I've thought this way about in years?

"We need to go. Enough dicking around, Lorelei." I hate my voice when I say it. It doesn't sound like I'm taking her to jail. It sounds like I'm begging her to get on her knees and take my cock into her mouth.

She doesn't notice my voice or my dark eyes. She stands and drains her own cup. "I need to put Bogey back in the kennel."

I look down at the dog wagging his tail at Lorelei's feet and looking up at her like she's a goddess. The dog watches her like I'd like to look at her if she wasn't who she is and I wasn't who I am.

I also like the damn dog and don't want him to have to go back into his kennel. "Does he like car rides?"

She bends down and kisses him on his nose, and I've never been so jealous of a dog. "He loves them. Don't you Bogey?" she coos.

"Let's bring him. We need to process you, but you'll be free to go after that. He can ride in the car, and I'll bring you home."

"I'm pretty sure that's not how it usually works," she says.

I chuckle, and my laughter makes Lorelei turn her head like she's watching something interesting. Then again, I've probably never laughed around her. "What about tonight has been normal?"

"You don't take other busts to your mom's and then come back to their house for tea?"

"It's definitely been a first," I say, putting my hand on her lower back and guiding her out to my car.

I can't help but feel like my hand belongs there. Right on her back and supporting her.

"Whose dog is that?" Chase asks, throwing an apple down on his desk and nodding at the dog sitting dutifully in my lap.

"This is Bogey. Whatever you're going to say...don't."

"Is he a stray? Why does he look like he likes you?"

I put up my middle finger. "He's Lorelei Rogers's dog."

"The hot pot baker?" Chase says a little too loudly, looking around the cubicle area.

I almost spill Bogey onto the floor as I lean forward and make a shushing gesture. "Shut the fuck up!" I hiss. "She's here. I brought her in. If she hears that I think she's hot, I'll never hear the end of it, and I will beat you to death."

"You have weird date ideas, bro." He sits down and puts his feet on the desk.

"It's not a date. I caught her food truck of death and destruction on the public walkway."

Chase furrows his brow and purses his lips. "How far onto the public walkway?"

"Shut up." I look back at my file and run my hand down Bogey's black fur.

"A foot? Don't tell me you brought that wonderful, sexy goddess into the station for a foot."

I shift my legs uncomfortably under Bogey. He's part lab and part rottweiler and not the size of an average lapdog, but he insisted on curling up in as much of my lap as he could take. His head is propped on my desk since it didn't quite fit with the rest of his body.

"Half an inch," I mumble.

"Your dick is only half an inch? Sorry about that, but how much was she over the line?"

I stare at him, and I'm suddenly filled with shame that broils in my stomach and nauseates me. Even Chase is going to give me shit over this. "Half an inch."

It dawns on him, and he lets out a low whistle. "Well, it's safe to say you've ruined the entire department's chances with that one. Good job, asshole. I would have asked her out, and now I'll need to apologize for my dick partner."

"Fuck off. You weren't going to ask her out."

"I sure was. I looked her up on that website of hers."

"You're not asking her out."

"Don't get all holy with me. Pot's legal now. She's no different than the bartender you took home last year after Mardi Gras."

I flex my jaw and grit my teeth. "She's totally fucking different. Everything about her is different. You stay the fuck away from her!" I growl, jabbing a pen at him.

He puts his hands up like he's being robbed. "Whoa, soldier. Fine. Won't ask her out." An evil smile spreads across his face, and I look back at my laptop. "She's obviously already spoken for."

"She's single."

"Do you want her to be, though?"

I ruffle Bogey's fur and am rewarded with a long lick up my hand. I want to take this dog home, or at least ask Lorelei where she found him. He's exactly what I'd want if I got another dog. "I don't know what you're talking about."

"I think you know exactly what I'm talking about. You like her, don't you?"

"No, I don't."

"Yes, you do."

"Nuh-uh."

"Uh-huh," he drawls, nodding and biting his lip. "Are we going to throw out an 'I'm rubber and you're glue' next?"

I stare at my laptop and try to concentrate as Bogey wags his tail, hitting my thigh with it every few seconds. "We need to focus on this Lambert character," I say. I nod at the screen, and Chase stiffens. "I don't want to talk about Lorelei."

Chase takes the hint and straightens in his chair. Jacob Lambert is a meth dealer we've been after for almost a year. He doesn't do the cooking. Most meth users and dealers make their own since it's not something that people plan out. The entire meth operation is one born of desperation and scarce supplies. But Jacob Lambert has treated his meth organization like it's cocaine in the eighties. He has several cookers in locations all over the state and runners between all of them. He runs a true meth ring, and he operates his home base in our county.

Chase opens his laptop, Lorelei forgotten, and types in his credentials. For the next fifteen minutes, we discuss the movement of supplies and go over information from a couple of undercover guys. The undercover officers have infiltrated the organization, and we have six months of intel for us to go over. We're getting closer to getting him, and we're going to make our move against him soon.

Eventually, the door from the processing area opens, and Lorelei walks into the room. I flex my jaw and gnash my teeth when I see the young officer about Lorelei's age put his hand on her lower back to guide her to my cubicle. He's smiling like they're new best friends, and I want to punch the smile off his face.

Lorelei throws her head back mid-walk and stops to grab the officer's arm. She laughs, and the sound makes every head turn. "Your girl's here," Chase mutters under his breath just as Bogey stands on my lap and yaps.

"There's my boy!" Lorelei coos in my direction, and my heart speeds up. It takes a moment to realize she's talking to Bogey and not me. The smile on my face isn't lost on Chase, and he snorts.

I ignore him. "Are you ready to go home?" I ask.

"I can take her," the officer walking with her says. "It's on my beat. We just came for the dog."

I nail him with a glare that he doesn't understand. He doesn't even blink. "I'll take her home."

"It's on the way," he says, still not understanding. He points over his shoulder.

"I love that I have two big, strong men willing to take me home," Lorelei giggles. She runs her hand up the other officer's bicep, and I bite down so hard I think my teeth will crack. "There's enough of me to go around, gentlemen."

No, there God damn is not. I don't want her touching his bicep or any other man's bicep. I want my bicep to be the only one she touches. I know it's ridiculous to feel that way after I've spent the last week harassing her business, but something about talking to her tonight and getting to know her has me already jealous of any man that would get to spend time with her.

I need to out-alpha this beat cop. "I'm heading out. I will take her, officer." I drag out the last word, throwing my rank as a lieutenant on the drug task force over the beat officer.

He finally catches on, and the poor sap deflates in front of me. His shoulders slouch, a frown furrowing his face. He turns to Lorelei and gives her puppy dog eyes. "It was nice to meet you, even if I had to take your mug shot. Do you want to hang out or something? Dinner?"

"Bogey has to shit!" I yell louder than necessary. I grab Lorelei's arm and spin her toward the door as I grab Bogey's leash. Thankfully, the dog dutifully comes along with me. "Better get going before we have another mess on the carpet."

"If you're referring to that burrito night incident, that's unfair," Chase replies, kicking his feet back on his desk with a coy smile. I glower at him before quickly walking Lorelei and Bogey out to my car, worrying the whole way about how I'll say goodbye to her when I get her home.

Chapter 10

LORELEI

"Did he kiss you goodnight when he walked you to the porch?" Kailee asks, wiping her hair back and taking a sip of her topped-off margarita, her third of the night.

Thank fuck for Saturday night margaritas at The Vault, a quaint bar in town that specializes in good drinks without the loud music or bad acoustics. You can hear yourself talk in here, and the booths and bar stools are usually full of other Saturday workers coming off of shifts and hanging out with coworkers. The Vault is hot with retail workers, musicians done with a set, and even the odd policeman or fireman coming off their shift. Kailee and I are at our usual spots at the bar. The bartender, Joey, saves our seats for us every Saturday after we close up the truck at whatever concert we've been working.

I half expected Liam to show up to the hairband concert tonight and flip his tape measure out at me. The problem is, I was actually looking for him. I wanted to see him, even if it was to harass me, and there's been a disappointment lodged in my stomach that I haven't seen him all night.

"He walked me to the door and made sure I was inside before we did this awkward stare down through the screen door."

Kailee looks up and licks a spot of salt from her top lip. "Like when we were teens and guys would be unsure if they should kiss us before we went inside?"

A sigh escapes my chest before I can stop it, and it sounds like a swoon. "That's exactly what it felt like. It was like that nervous flutter you feel in your chest, but you know they're nervous, too. He wouldn't meet my eyes, seemed more interested in my dog, and acted like he didn't know what to do with his hands," I chuckle, remembering how Liam stuck his hands in his pockets, ruffled his hair, and then moved his hands back to his pockets. "Maybe I'm wrong, though. He may have just been making sure I was safe."

"Did you want to kiss him?" Kailee asks. She has the uncanny ability to see right through me, and I know she already knows the answer. No use lying to her.

"I did." I blow out a breath and slouch onto the bar, resting my head on the mahogany. "I can't get him out of my head. I was disappointed I didn't get to spar with him tonight or even see him. He didn't come by, and I really wanted him to, Kailee. Why him, though? What makes him so special? All he's done is give me shit and make my first mugshots possible."

"You read romance. You know women like it when shit isn't easy. He's not easy."

I pick my head up and focus my eyes on her. "Oh, I think he's easy."

"Really?" she drawls. "You think you could get him into bed?"

"Oh, I know I could."

Kailee reaches into the bowl of pretzels on the table and grabs a bite, chews, and swallows while watching me through squinted eyes. "Let's put a wager on it."

"Excuse me? Are you betting if I can fuck the hot, mean cop?"

"Is he really mean?"

I slouch and bang my forehead on the bar, grinding it into the wood a little with a groan. Maybe I should slow down on the margaritas. "That's the thing. I don't feel like he is. Sure, he doesn't like drugs, even legal ones, but I think he's nice. He loves his mom. To be honest, his mom is really lovable, though. He likes Bogey, and Bogey likes him. Bogey doesn't like everyone, so that tells me that he's a good guy."

"Dogs are never wrong."

We drink in silence for a moment, Kailee sipping her margarita and me drinking the dregs of mine and waving for Joey to bring me another. "Fifty bucks," Kailee mumbles.

"That's an expensive margarita."

"No, fifty bucks you can't lay the good officer. Hell, I got twenty you can't work up the balls to even kiss him."

I place my margarita glass on the bar and shove it so Joey can pick it up and wash it. "I'll take the twenty-dollar bet. I can't do the fifty."

"Why not?"

"If I fuck him, I don't want it to be for money. I want it to be because we're arguing and he captures my mouth in a warm kiss as his hands roam up to my breasts," I say, trailing my hands over my body and causing Kailee to almost spit out her drink in laughter. "You know, like in my books I read. His mom reads those, by the way. Maybe Liam's read one or two and knows how to bend a good woman over and take her like a true alpha male."

Kailee stops laughing and straightens up suddenly, the picture of sobriety. Her eyes flit behind me for a second, and a smile lights up her face as she focuses her eyes on my face again. "Wouldn't that be funny if you did take the bet? The upstanding, angelic drug task force officer helping you seal a fifty-dollar bet with sex is downright tawdry. It would also be ironic."

"Why would it be ironic?"

Kailee smiles and covers her hand with mine. "Focus on my face and laugh in another ten seconds."

"What's going on?"

"Just do it."

I do as she asks and then chuckle loudly in a fake laugh that gives away that I've had a couple of margaritas tonight. In fact, we sound like immature high school girls. Kailee ends the laugh with a snort and signals for Joey to get her yet another drink.

"What the fuck was that about?" I ask.

Kailee holds up a finger. "Let me get another drink first so I can fully enjoy the irony and shenanigans."

"What?"

"Officer Half Inch just walked in with a sex god I wouldn't mind collecting fifty bucks for and is about twenty feet behind you."

I start to turn around, and Kailee grabs my arm. "Don't look. He'll see you!"

"You just wanted to bet me to kiss him, and now you don't want me to even look at him. Christ, make up your mind."

"I was joking about the bet."

I wasn't, but that's not the point here.

"Is he with a girl?" I ask, a horrible thought coming into my mind. I don't think I could stand it if he was on a double date or something.

Familiar butterflies take flight in my stomach, and the back of my neck feels hot. I take deep breaths. There's no way I can even sneak out of the bar because he's between us and the door. My eyes flick to the back of the bar near the restrooms and wonder if there's a back door to this place. There has to be another door in case of a fire or something, right?

But why leave? I was upset I didn't get to see him tonight, so why am I nervous? Hell, he doesn't know I'm here unless he installed a tracking device on my car and is stalking me. He's just here for a drink. A normal guy on the town with one of his friends or something.

"Does he look hot?" I ask, and I immediately grimace. I sound like I wasn't at school today and am asking my friend what my crush wore.

Kailee has the same impression. "Want me to pass him a note in the shape of a football?"

"May as well since you won't even let me turn around and look at him, much less go over and talk to him."

She squares her shoulders back and turns to face the bar. "Fine. Go talk to him. Maybe you can harass him while you're over there."

"Don't threaten me with a good time," I say, placing my drink on the bar a little harder than necessary and straightening my posture. "Do I look good enough to go over there? There's no lipstick on my teeth, right?"

"You look fierce," Kailee says, eyeing my tight jeans, blue sequin tank top, and gold butterfly necklace that hangs down to my cleavage. I'm in full makeup, and grab my gloss out of my purse, swiping it on my lips before I stand up with purpose.

"I'm going to go over there. Wish me luck."

I don't give her a chance to speak. I turn and stop short as I take in what Liam looks like out of his officer work outfit.

Fuck me.

He leisurely leans against the bar in dark jeans and a black golf shirt with a button undone at the top. It's enough for me to see a speck of dark chest hair, but I'm too busy drooling at how well the shirt fits over his pecs and torso. This is no dress shirt he wears for work, and it shows every line of his muscles. His skin is tan like he played a round of golf today, hence the shirt, or he was out on a leisurely boat ride.

The son of a bitch is actually smiling a full smile, and he looks like a different person. At ease. Happy. There's no woman in sight, thank fuck, and he's talking to his blond guy friend that I saw at the station. That must be his partner, but I don't have time to care right now because I'm too busy thinking about Liam's hands and the way he holds his beer. I can't help but wish his fingers were wrapped around my thighs like that. I've never been so jealous of a beer stein in my life as he brings the rim to his lips and slurps foam off the top. I'd love for my nipples to be that foam.

I take two steps, and the mood in the room changes. His eyes roam over my face, and he does a double take. I swear the chatter in the bar stops, or I just go temporarily deaf as he blinks twice at me and tilts his head like he's not sure if I'm real.

I can do this. I paste a smile on my face, toss my hair, and stride right over to Liam. "Fancy seeing you here, Officer Half Inch."

Liam's partner spits out a mouthful of beer and starts cackling, but Liam ignores him. "Thanks for that. I'll never get rid of that nickname now," Liam says, throwing the pretzel that was in his fist down on the bar.

"You deserve that in life."

"What are you doing here?" he asks, looking behind me and jerking his chin at Kailee.

"I could ask the same question since it's almost like you're stalking me."

"I'm not stalking you. I came here for a drink."

"Legal drugs, huh?"

"I'm sorry?"

"You're enjoying legal drugs. Alcohol is a drug, technically, and it's legal. Just like my goodies."

He laughs a little and shifts his posture so that he's taller. Damn near intimidating. "Your goodies?"

"You've seen my goodies. Last night."

Liam's face reddens right as his partner inhales beside me. "Just out of curiosity, what kind of goodies did my stick-in-the-butt partner see last night after he dropped you off?" his partner asks. "I'm Chase, by the way."

I shake Chase's outstretched hand but don't look away from Liam who fidgets like he's uncomfortable, but he meets my eyes. I'll give him that.

"Oh, he saw all my goodies in my greenhouse. Didn't you, Liam? You wanted to burn those goodies down. Touch them. Put your dirty fingers on them."

"What do you want, Lorelei?" he mumbles.

I reach into my purse and pull out the white package I got at a pot shop earlier in the week. Thankfully, it's still in the original packaging with the sticker attached so I can have it sealed in public, and I wave the small box under Liam's nose. "Oh, I was just on my way home to enjoy some of the pre-rolled herbal remedies I got the other day. See," I say, waving it back in front of him and pointing to the sticker on the white box. "Marijuana. Here's me wafting marijuana under a drug task force agent's nose in a proper container, and you can't do anything about it. Weeeeed." I cackle like I'm a witch and wave it like I'm hypnotizing Liam. "Look at the evil weed in front of your face."

He catches my hand and pushes my wrist down. "Are you drunk, Lorelei?"

"I've only had a couple of margaritas." I don't think I'm drunk. Holy shit, am I drunk? Now that I think about it, I have to be sloshed to come over to him, talk to him, and wave pre-rolled joints in front of his face. Maybe the third margarita was a bad idea.

I put the joints back in my purse, suddenly wanting nothing but to slink back over to Kailee and ignore him. "Um, okie dokie. It's good to see you." I turn to Chase. "Nice to meet you. You seem nice. More fun than your partner. But I'm going to go back to my friend now."

I turn to go back to Kailee, but a hand reaches out and grabs my wrist. "Where are you going? I thought you were going home to smoke the death sticks?"

I whirl back around, a sneer on my face. "Don't like me walking away, huh? I've actually changed my mind. I'm leaving. That way, we don't have to see each other."

I wave to Kailee over my shoulder and duck under Liam's arm, stalking toward the door. He turns and follows me, hot on my heels. I reach to open the door to the bar, and Liam puts his hand over it. "You're not driving like this."

I spin around to face him again and find his nose an inch from mine. He doesn't back up, and I can smell the one drink of beer he probably got to have before I interrupted his night. I could stand on my tip toes and kiss him, but I don't. I just stare at his lips as they slightly part like he wants to say something, but I beat him to it.

"Why do you always try to babysit me? I don't need a life boss."

"You obviously do. You need a babysitter. Actually, what you need is a good spanking, but that would be an inappropriate use of my position."

Heat moves from my chest all the way down to my toes, and a mental picture of bending over Liam's lap as those masculine hands come down on my tender skin flashes through my mind. I gasp a little, which is a terrible choice because I breathe in every bit of his Liam scent.

"You wouldn't," I mumble.

"Oh, I would, drug dealer. But what you need now is a ride home, so I'm going to drive your troublesome ass home for the second night in a row."

"I refuse."

"I can drive you home, or you can leave and I can call in a report of a drunk driver. You can go to the station for a second night. Which do you want?"

I look over my shoulder and find Kailee, still sitting at the bar, making a humping motion with her arms and licking her lips. I shake my head a little at her and she brings her hands to her mouth, making a blow job action as she pushes her tongue against her cheek. I give her the finger, and that just makes her turn her back to me, cross her arms around her back, and bob her head like she's making out with someone.

With friends like her, who needs enemies?

Liam turns to Chase, gives him a finger that isn't the middle one I just flashed at Kailee, and Chase nods, probably understanding that Liam will drop me off and be right back. "Come on," he says. "I'll run you home."

I let him turn my shoulders, open the door for me, and put that damn hand at my lower back to walk me to his car. This time, he escorts me to the front seat like I'm a model citizen, tenderly buckles my seatbelt for me, and gently shuts the door like he's taking me to dinner.

Chapter 11

LIAM

"Do you always need help with your keys?" I ask as Lorelei misses the keyhole twice before jamming the key inside the lock. "I've never seen you get it on one try."

"It was the handcuffs last night. My hand is shaking tonight. Cut me a break. Are you going to insult me all night?"

"Still drunk?"

"Oddly, no. It took longer to get here with traffic. I'm just thirsty."

I'd like to walk her into the house, get her a glass of water, and tuck her into bed so I know she's safe and can't inflict trouble on civilized society. I try to push aside the thoughts that I'd like to get into bed with her to make sure she stays out of trouble, but I can't let her suck me into her life of depravity.

Eventually, the door opens, and Lorelei walks into the living room, plopping on the couch like she's exhausted. Maybe she is. I look at my black watch and notice it's way past midnight. Somewhere in the back of the house, Bogey barks, and I don't wait for permission. I walk to the utility room and let him out of his kennel, his tail wagging so violently it slaps his flank. "Hi, buddy," I mumble as he stands on his hind legs.

I pat his head and stare at him. Is he begging for a treat? He drops to the floor for a moment and then gets on his back legs again, his tongue lolling to the side and whimpering. "Is there something wrong with your dog?" I yell. "He's being weird."

Lorelei obviously isn't drunk because she runs into the utility room with a concerned look on her face. It doesn't last long, and her smile lights up the room when she sees Bogey. "He wants his hug."

"His what?" I ask, looking back at the dog, who is now hopping around on his hind legs.

"His puppy hug. Here," she says, pushing me to the side, bending down, and wrapping her arms around Bogey. She strokes his head and rubs her cheek against the side of his face. "See. He wants a hug. I've never seen him ask for a hug from anyone but me." She stands up, and her eyes take a second to focus. "He must not think you're the terrible tool you've been to me."

"Terrible tool?" I ask, but she doesn't answer. Bogey gets on his hind legs in front of me and whines.

"Go ahead. Hug him if you want."

I bend down and wrap my arms around my drug nemesis's dog, and he licks the side of my face. I can't help it - I giggle, which causes Lorelei to laugh, causing my dick to twitch against my pants.

I made her laugh, and I'd give my left ring finger to hear it again because of something I said or did. I'd give anything to make her happy. If I only thought she'd give up her ridiculous and unethical career choice, I could come home every night and hug this dog. Hug Lorelei. Kiss her, even. What would it be like to come home and make love to her after a dinner I make for her or after watching a show together?

I look at her feet, imagining them in my lap and perilously close to my...

"Who's my big boy?" she asks, and she's talking to the damn dog again.

Fuck if I don't want her to say that to me. Just once.

I set Bogey down, and he runs for his leash to go outside. "Go get some water or make yourself some coffee. I'll take him out," I say.

"You will?" She eyes Bogey and looks back at me. "You really like him, huh? How do I know you won't steal him?"

"I guess you'll just have to trust me on that one."

She doesn't argue this time, and I quickly take Bogey outside and dispose of his business before coming back into the house to find Lorelei brewing a cup of coffee in her coffee pot.

Her going-out clothes are gone, replaced by pajamas. Her bare toes wiggle against the clean linoleum, and my eyes run the length of her tan, long legs, stopping long enough to admire her plaid pajama shorts that barely cover her ass. She's in a tight, spaghetti-strap tank, and her hair is in a messy bun with tendrils free and hanging down her neck.

"I need to go," I say, jerking my thumb over my shoulder.

"Stay for a cup."

"I told Chase I'd be right back."

"Kailee will keep him company."

"Oh, dear Lord," I mumble, running my hands through my hair. "We left our hot, irresponsible friends together."

"Yeah, that just crossed your mind, huh? I bet they aren't even there right now. He totally bailed on you, and they're probably rolling around Kailee's living room floor naked as we speak."

She passes me a cup of black coffee and waits for another cup to brew from the individual coffee pot. "Why were you at the bar?" she asks, no longer slurring. She's definitely sober enough for a conversation. "Entrapment? Undercover sting for jaywalkers outside?"

I take a sip of the coffee and set it back down. "You know, Lorelei, I'm just going to go if this is going to be weird between us. I'm a good officer. You're a pot baker. I'm doing my job. Maybe I've been...overzealous at bringing you in, but I'm a good cop."

"Overzealous?" she shrieks. "I've never even had an overdue library book, Officer Lane." The way she says the word is choppy. She pronounces every syllable like my name is filth. "Then you come along, and I've been fined and taken to the police station for doing something that is legal now and makes people happy, whether you like it or not."

She leans over the counter and jabs her index finger in my face, and I half want to put it in my mouth and suck on it before biting it off. Never, in my thirty-three years on this infernal planet, have I ever disliked someone so much and wanted to peel their panties off with my teeth at the same time.

"Your coffee's ready," I growl, not blinking, as her cup fills behind her.

"I don't fucking care!" she yells. "Mugshots, Liam! I've had mugshots and fingerprints because you're butthurt about me." She spins around and grabs her coffee off the coffee maker, flips me the middle finger, and drinks a huge gulp of what has to be scalding liquid. "You really should get a life and stop being obsessed with mine," she says, placing the cup down so hard that coffee sloshes onto the counter.

That's a punch to the dick. I'm well aware I don't have a life, but I don't need a drug seller to rub it in. What the hell is she playing at, anyway? Offering me coffee just to yell at me?

"At least my life doesn't involve drugs."

"Well, you're a drug agent, so it kind of does. But that's it, right? Dinner with your mommy once a week and a sad job you get to use for a power trip."

I push my coffee cup back and get up from her stool so fast it falls behind me. I huff out of the room as she laughs behind me, taunting me. "Sure, walk away, Officer Half Inch."

I won't leave like this. Not when she's laughing at my lack of social life or the fact that I just do my job. I spin around and walk back to her, my boots heavy on her floor and the only sound in the room.

As I get close, her eyes widen, and she backs up until she backs into her kitchen counter, the steam from the coffee pot still rising behind her.

Sheer depravity washes over me. Lust. Anger. Disappointment with myself. Disappointment at an amazing woman like her choosing to sell drugs and taunt me with it. My hands flex at my sides, and I push my forehead into hers, her skin hot against mine. I almost let my eyes flutter closed and lean into it, but I keep my eyes open and stare at her as she blinks at the proximity of me. I can see the length of her lashes and small flecks of green in her eyes.

"Fuck you, Lorelei Rogers," I whisper. "You think you know me so well? You're just a drug seller that could be so much more. You could have your own shop and sell respectable baked goods, but you choose to sell poison, something you could have gone to jail for a year ago."

"You're not the boss of my life," she whispers back, and her nose touches mine. I could kiss her now. I could just bend down a little more and drop my lips to hers. Damn, I wonder what she tastes like. "You can't punish me the way you want. I'm so fucking sorry you can't send me to jail for life for selling pot brownies."

I bring my hand to her throat, and she flinches before covering my hand with her fingers. She runs her thumb over my hand, and the innocent gesture nearly makes my core explode with the heat moving from my dick to every inch of my body. "If you think I want to see you in an orange jumpsuit and behind bars, you're wrong, sweetheart. And you're also wrong about the punishment. I can punish you, Lorelei."

"What are you going to do, Liam? Take me to jail again? Kiss me to punish me?" She laughs, and it's a hard sound.

The laughter stops suddenly, and she nuzzles my cheek. "Am I your temptation, Liam? Do you want to be bad with me? Just a little? Just to see what the dark side is like?" She pulls back and runs her tongue up my cheek, humming as she tastes the salt in my skin. "Do it, you fucking coward."

A cross between a chuckle and growl escapes my mouth, and I move my mouth to her ear, leaning in for a whisper and searching for the words I've wanted to say since I first saw her leaning out of the damn truck window.

"Not tonight, Lorelei," I coo and stroke the tip of her chin with my finger. "I won't give you the satisfaction of kissing you and you thinking you're getting a nice goodnight kiss from a nice cop."

She trembles under me, but I spin her around before she can sink to her knees. The way her legs move, they're Jell-O, and that's not my endgame tonight. One day, I'd like her on her knees in front of me, my hands in her hair as I fuck her mouth.

Just not tonight.

Tonight, I'm going to punish her like I've wanted to for days.

I push myself against her body, and she arches into me. "Liam," she whines, her hand coming to my shoulder.

I ignore her sound, even though I yearn to kiss that whine away from her lips. I push her so she's bent over the counter and pull her pants down in one movement, her shorts and panties dropping to the floor at her ankles.

She doesn't cover herself. There's no push against me. She sinks into the counter and grips the grouted tile above her head, knocking over the dish soap dispenser and sending it rolling across the granite. She spreads her legs a little like she's accepting anything I have a mind to slip in there.

And that ass. Fuck me. It's round, full, and the pale skin begs to be reddened by my hand or belt.

I run my hand up her back like I'm soothing a wild animal. Let's be honest, I am. If there's any woman I've met that could be called a wild beast, it's Lorelei Rogers.

"W-What are you going to do to me, Officer Lane?"

My hand runs up her back again, liking the feel of her skin under me, and I grab her entire messy bun in my fist as my other hand moves to my belt buckle. "I'm going to punish you how you deserve."

Chapter 12

LORELEI

Punish me?

A trickle of wetness runs down my thighs, and I'm not sure if it's sweat or my body's excitement at the idea of my bare ass exposed to Liam. I'd give anything to know what he's thinking right now.

His warm fingers move down my body, and I tremble. I bend further over the counter until my nose touches the cool hardness because my legs won't support me. Without the kitchen counter, I wouldn't be able to stand.

"H-how do you think I deserve to be p-punished?" I stammer, my top lip suddenly stiff, and my bottom lip trembling with the rest of my body.

He doesn't answer. I'm frozen and don't move my head to look back, but my ears still work. The sound of his belt buckle coming undone and the leather sliding through the belt loops on his jeans makes my legs buckle, and I sigh.

Is he going to fuck me? Dear Christ, please let him fuck me. Please.

I arch my back and present my ass to him, widening my stance so he can get to any hole he wants to touch. My eyes flit to my countertop in the hopes that if he chooses my ass, he'll at least look for the coconut oil first.

Before I can think further, he bunches his belt in his hand and sets it on the counter two inches from my face. I open my left eye only to see his masculine hand splayed on the counter by my cheek, belt in hand, and his biceps tremble as he leans over me. His erection rests against my butt crack, and he moves his lips to my ear. "I think you know what I'm going to do to punish you. I just thought you'd like to see the belt I'm going to punish you with."

Fuck me. I've never been spanked before, but I read about it in books. I've always wanted to try it in the confines of a nice relationship, the kind of relationship where everything is equal out of the bedroom but there's nothing but dirty, disrespectful sex in the bedroom.

Or kitchen, as it seems.

"Lick it," he orders next to my cheek.

"What? Your dick?"

He chuckles into my skin, and his breath hits my earlobe. "No, Lorelei. Lick the belt before I spank you with it."

Bitch, do not ask me to show off if you don't want me to show off. "Officer Lane, are you threatening me with a good time?"

"Lick the belt," he whispers, grinding his dick into my ass and pressing his cock between my butt cheeks.

Time to show my ass figuratively, even if I'm already doing it literally.

I turn my head as much as I can while keeping my ear to the granite. His damn brown eyes meet mine, and I hold eye contact. As much as I want to look away, I won't give him that power.

He gasps as he breathes, and I can tell he's keeping his shoulders as still as he can, not wanting to show me that he's literally panting over my helpless body.

Tentatively, I stick out my tongue and drag it the length of his belt. I take one swipe up the leather, swipe back down like it's a damn lollipop, and go back up before spitting on his belt buckle to either show disrespect…or that I'm a dirty whore. I'll leave that for him to interpret.

His eyes darken above me, and his thighs tremble against the backs of mine. "Lorelei," he whispers without moving his slightly parted lips.

Because I'm trouble on wheels and want to give him hell, I drag my tongue over the leather one more time, flicking my tongue over each hole as I pass them, and move my tongue to the webbing between his index finger and thumb.

My eyes flutter when I taste his skin. His hand is a salty shock to my taste buds after the cold, tasteless leather of his belt.

He straightens as I close my eyes, and he takes the belt with him. He mutters something that sounds like "trouble and filthy to boot," but I can't be sure.

My fingers flex against the countertop, bracing myself for what's coming, and I don't wait long.

The leather practically whistles through the air, so I hear the belt a millisecond before it strikes. The leather comes down so hard that I buck into the handle of the cabinet below me, and the metal digs into my leg. He doesn't give me time to adjust, or maybe he just doesn't notice. Something tells me he'd move me if he thought I was getting hurt in another way other than what he's inflicting.

The belt whistles through the air again. This time, I take in the cracking sound of it hitting my buttocks as searing pain shoots through my entire lower body.

Oh, but what pain it is. Exquisite. Sexual.

I want more, and I spread my legs against my better judgment. A growl comes from his chest as he grips my bun harder and pulls up so I can't rest my head on the counter. I close my eyes and savor the pain at my scalp – just enough to feel dominated – and the burning pain of my ass that's going to be a bitch tomorrow.

I can't get enough today, though.

"Had enough, Lorelei?" he whispers. His voice is strange, and I wonder if he's worried he really hurt me.

"You hit like a little bitch, Liam," I chuckle. "I thought you said you wanted to punish me."

He hits me harder, and a few dribbles of urine leak out of me from the pressure. This time, he notices what's going on at my front as the urine dribbles into my shorts at my ankles.

I ignore it, though. This is the most erotic moment of my life, and my clit is on fire, begging to be touched. I'll be damned if I let a little urine that squeezed out ruin my night with him.

He throws his belt on the counter and sighs as he runs those warm, soft hands over my ass, rubbing the pain or redness away. Disappointment pushes my shoulders into a slouch, and I whimper as I look at the belt on my counter.

He pushes me forward again and brings his hand to my ass this time, eliciting a giggle from me.

He pauses, and the room goes silent. "Are you kidding me right now? How hard do I have to spank you to be considered punishment?"

I bite my lip and look around at him again. Sweat dots his forehead, and he doesn't even try to hide his panting. "Maybe Daddy should have me go out back and pick out my own switch?"

His face reddens, and his eyes widen while I laugh like the devil and turn around to face my kitchen tile. "I was hoping I'd see some real action from you tonight, Officer Lane."

He pushes on the back of my neck and holds me down to the granite. I push against him, trying to rise, but it's futile. His hand is like a vice at the back of my neck, and I knew those sexy hands would be strong. "Touch yourself, Lorelei," he whispers. "I know you want to, and I want to watch you touch yourself."

I bring my right hand to my clit without having to be asked a second time. At the same time, I hear Liam unzip his pants. "Yes," I moan under him.

"Are you moaning because you're that good with your fingers, or are you moaning because you think I'm going to do something for you?"

"Both are fun ideas," I taunt.

"I've never met such a disturbed, filthy, foul-mouthed creature, Ms. Rogers."

"And I've never met a man that pretended so hard that he wasn't into it."

Silence hangs between us for a few moments until the sound of his pants moving to his knees startles me. He keeps the hand at the back of my neck as I furiously run my fingers in the clockwise pattern I know my body likes. He breathes hard and utters words like *beautiful, infernal*, and *the devil herself* as he does something behind me.

It takes a moment to realize that he's pleasuring himself as I'm pleasuring myself. "Are you going to just jerk off when you can have the real thing, Lane?"

"What makes you think I want to give you the satisfaction of fucking you?"

"Oh, I think you do want the satisfaction. I think you want to slide into my wet pussy and have your way with it. Just once."

"No."

"Come on, Liam. Is this where I beg *you* to just put the tip in?"

"Beg all you want. You aren't getting fucked tonight. If you want to come, you'll do it yourself."

If he was running his hand along his dick quietly before, he speeds up so I can hear every jerk of his cock now. The sound makes me laugh. "You know I can run my tongue up your dick like I did to that belt if you let me turn around."

I turn to look at him as much as I can with his hand still holding me down at the back of my neck. His mouth opens in a silent moan, and he pushes his cock into my butt crack. He bites his lip, whimpers, and then squares his shoulders like he's doing everything he can to hold his ever-loving shit together.

"Maybe just the tip on you won't hurt," he mutters.

He pushes himself slightly between my butt cheeks so I feel his cock on my puckered asshole. I've never done anal before. I was totally kidding to myself that I'd be fine with whatever hole he chose, and I grip the counter again, frantically grabbing my dish sponge and squeezing it like it's my best friend's hand.

He doesn't push in, though. He leaves the head of his cock pushed up against my asshole, but he doesn't enter me. I breathe out a sigh of relief and focus on my fingers as they expertly move over my clit. I take in every sigh he makes as he jerks himself off up against my asshole, and the sounds push me over the edge. I'd give anything to make him outright moan, to hear him call my name, but he seems hell bent to not give me that power.

I'll take my own power.

Pleasure moves from my clit to my core and out to my arms and legs. I drop the sponge, go limp under his hand, and he pushes me further against the counter to keep me from falling.

I won't call his name as I come. I refuse. This is a man that fucks with my business and thinks I'm an awful person. I may want to hear him moan for me, but I won't give him the satisfaction of moaning for him.

My orgasm comes in waves, and I tremble and whine below him, bucking my hips into the same cabinet handle that I was trying to avoid.

As soon as I'm finished, the hand pumping his cock moves faster, and pressure increases against my ass. He widens his strong legs and fucks his hand harder against me. He grits his teeth so hard they may crack, and his eyes squeeze shut. His thighs tremble one last time against mine as warm liquid covers my asshole and fills my crack.

Normally, I'd be disgusted, but that was the hottest way I've ever had a guy come for me.

As soon as every drop is out of him and dripping onto my shorts and kitchen floor, he moves back from me, pulling his pants up so I can't even see if the half inch taunting is earned.

He backs away from me, turns, takes a drink from his coffee, and walks out of the room, running a hand through his hair as he goes.

As soon as he's out the door, I pull up my shorts from around my ankles, take a sip from my now-cold coffee, and burst into tears. I don't cry because I was just spanked or treated like an easy jerkoff toy. I cry because I liked it and want him to stay. I want him to pull me into that broad, warm chest and wrap his arms around me.

Chapter 13

LIAM

"What the fuck is wrong with you tonight?" Chase huffs, blowing on his takeout box of steamy Chinese noodles.

As irresponsible as it is, we called for food delivery on a stakeout and had the owner bring it to us in the car. It's the little perks you get after you save someone's son from a heroin overdose and arrest the person that supplied the drugs to their kid. Mr. Lau now delivers noodles any time we call and has delivered in some pretty interesting locations, even waiving the delivery fee to creepy vans in creepy warehouse districts.

"Nothing," I growl, pushing a pork eggroll into my mouth and chewing with a little more force than usual.

Both of us stare straight ahead at Jacob Lambert's house. Actually, we stare at his driveway. Thankfully, the dickbag lives on a cul de sac that allows us to park where we can see his driveway, but we're not visible from the street. Even as I chew, a white sedan approaches the driveway, flashes its lights, and Jacob's younger brother, a fifteen-year-old kid named Carlton, comes out and hands the man a bag, receiving an envelope back. Carlton shoves it in his pocket as Chase adjusts the dash cam and takes pictures of the sedan's license plate.

"This is frustrating as all fuck."

"That you're in love with a pot baker?"

I cough out a piece of food and take a drink of the iced green tea Mr. Lau threw in for free. "I'm not in love with her."

"Sure, bro," Chase says, placing the camera back on the dash as the car drives away.

"It's frustrating that we can't chase that guy down and pull him over or get Carlton on selling."

Chase sighs and looks at his food like he suddenly finds it gross. "I know, but we're just gathering intel right now. Watching and building a case." He rubs his eyebrows and starts eating again. "You know as well as I do that Jacob sends his brother to make the trade because he'll only get juvie. You also know we need way more info than what we've got to make a case that sticks. We watch. That's it."

"What's up your ass, anyway? You've been in a bad mood since last week at the bar, and you weren't even there when I came back."

"You were gone a long time."

"I ran into baseball traffic."

"Sure, man. Baseball," Chase snorts.

I take another bite of food. "Kailee was gone when I went back to the bar."

"Sounds like she went home," he says. He cranes his neck and bends forward like he's very interested in what's going on outside the window.

"Did she go home with you?"

"Even if she did, I never kiss and tell."

"So, you kissed her?"

"What happened with you and Lorelei Rogers?" he asks, squinting.

"Don't change the subject."

He ignores me, and I can tell I'm not getting any information tonight. Honestly, I don't give a fuck. I'm too exhausted and uneasy to even argue with my partner or pump him for information. But I'd bet the deed to my house that he and Kailee fucked.

He goes back to eating, and I watch the house, taking tentative sips of my tea. Minutes feel like hours on a stakeout, and I swear I've been sitting in this car for a month.

I can't take it any longer. I grind the heels of my hands into both eye sockets until it hurts. "Fuck!"

Chase startles, jostling his drink and dropping a crab Rangoon between his legs. He utters a curse and wipes cream cheese off his pants. "What? What's wrong? Did Jacob make us?" He looks out the window and fumbles with his binoculars as he brings them to his face.

"Nothing," I sigh. I pick up my fork again and shove rice into my mouth. "I did something bad."

Chase drops the binoculars and turns to me. "Does this involve your baker?"

"She's not my baker."

"What happened? Don't tell me you confessed your undying love."

"Worse."

"What's worse than that?" he asks.

"I came on her butthole."

The silence in the car is deafening until Chase sputters food back into his container and laughs. It's a full belly laugh, and he clutches his chest, leans forward, and bangs his forehead on the steering wheel. "You did what? Jesus, Lane, I thought you were going to tell me you finally kissed her."

"I've never kissed her." I chew my food and stare straight ahead, not meeting his eyes.

Chase holds his hand up. "Wait a second. You didn't kiss her?"

"No."

"How do you come on a woman's brown eye and get away with not having to kiss her? Teach me your ways."

"Fuck off."

"You already did...on Lorelei's stink star."

"Stink star?" I look at him, disgusted.

"You know, her chocolate pocket. The brown starfish."

"I fucking hate you."

I dip my fork back into my food but leave it there. I'm too frustrated to eat. Why did I leave her like that? Fuck me, but I wanted to put my arms around her and bury myself in her. It took every ounce of control in my body not to push into that pussy that was so ready for me, her back arched so that her ass stuck in the air. Her body is the epitome of lush perfection, and my mouth waters at the thought, having nothing to do with the food in front of me.

Damn, I wanted to kiss her and explore every inch of her mouth with my tongue. How the hell did I manage to fuck up our first erotic moment? I wanted to stay, talk to her, and learn everything there is to know about her before kissing every inch of her body.

"Was the sex good?"

Chase's question pulls me out of my thoughts of running my tongue up her thigh. "What?" I ask, blinking at him like I just realized he's in the car. "I didn't say I fucked her."

He squints and wrinkles his nose. "How did you come on her butthole then? Don't tell me it was on accident."

I stare at him and blink. "How do you come on someone's butthole by accident?"

"You could fall and land on her funny while she was naked. Then, you could have come from the excitement of finding yourself between her crack flaps."

"It wasn't like that." I dip my head into my sweatshirt, wanting to hide. "I was punishing her, and it just happened."

"How exactly were you punishing her?" he asks, his eyebrows halfway up his forehead.

I sip my drink and sniff before answering. "She deserves a spanking for what she does. I spanked her."

Chase shakes his head and looks forward. "You're into some shit. You going to spank Jacob when we catch him, or are you just going to come on his chocolate faucet?"

I ignore him, even if I want to laugh at the bastard. We eat in silence for another minute as Chase shakes his head. "You like her, huh?" he finally asks when the silence gets to be unbearable.

I run my hand through my hair and crack the door open for some air. The keys in the ignition make the car door chime while it's open. "I don't know if I like her or want to strangle her. Most of the time, I experience both feelings in her presence."

"Sounds like love to me."

"Doesn't matter. I probably fucked up any chance I had with her." I stop myself and turn to Chase. "Not that I want a chance with her. She's into drugs and sells them, for fuck's sake."

He chuckles. "Want to know what I think?"

"Not particularly, but since we're stuck in this car, you're probably going to tell me."

"I think you like her, and I think she likes you. I've never seen your eyes look like they do when you look at her. She does something to you, man."

"Yeah, she gives me indigestion." I stare out the window for a few seconds. "I'm curious. What do my eyes look like when she's around?"

"They look like you're a lovesick fool who thinks the only way to get the girl to pay attention to him is to pop her bra between math and study hall." He puts his hand on the back of my headrest and turns to face me. "I have to know. Are you really that worried about pot brownies?"

"It's a threat to society."

He smirks. "Is it really? I mean, this guy is a threat to society." He nods at Jacob's house just as another light flashes and another vehicle, this one a pickup truck, rolls up to the house.

Chase and I both take our pictures and document the exchange, the time, and the vehicle's information. Chase runs the license plate through our computer system, and we document the owner's name and address. All of this is crucial to get the proper warrants and build a case. Even though the person in the truck is buying drugs, they're not our big fish to fry and can often provide us with information when they think that information can save their own ass. Sometimes, a visit from the police asking for information about the drug seller can scare someone into rehab or changing their ways. We need cause to get a warrant to enter the house, especially with a minor present.

Chase finishes the pictures, and I file an index card with time and info into Jacob's file, a failsafe in case our computer information disappears. It's happened before in our office, and my department has learned to save information in more than one place.

Chase is right about Lorelei. The dick munch we're staking out is the real deal. Lorelei is sweet, kind, beautiful, and a good dog owner. I had a real chance with her before I fucked it up by issuing her fines and putting handcuffs on her. To make matters worse, she has to go to a court hearing in a couple of weeks to discuss the case and receive the formal fine and strike against her record. It's not a real court case with a jury and everything, but she has to talk to the judge and bring a lawyer.

Fuck, I made the woman I'm obsessed with have to pay for a lawyer and take time to go to the courthouse.

"How do I make this up to her, man?"

Chase shrugs. "Take her out on a date."

"How? I can't just walk up to her door and ask her out. I could get her phone number from the system, but that would get me in trouble or look bad."

"You could also go to the truck at her next event."

I stare out the window. Can I eat shit enough to be vulnerable and ask her out like I haven't tried to ruin her business and happiness all at once?

Chapter 14

Lorelei

"So, you've never kissed the guy, but you let him come on your asshole?" Kailee asks, popping a fresh batch of banana bread into the storage cooler. "That seems a little backward. Coming on assholes is usually second-date stuff."

"What kind of second dates do you go on?" I ask.

"The fun kind." Kailee shakes her shoulders and bites her lip. I give her an annoyed look and go back to setting my mixer to mix more bananas, flour, sugar, and infused butter. She stiffens and grows serious. "Here's the million-dollar question. Did you want to kiss him?"

"I did," I grumble. "I can't help it, Kailee. I wanted to turn around, slide my arms up his chest and around that neck I'd like to wring, and kiss the hell out of him."

I'm not lying. I've thought about it for over a week. What would it be like to finally know what Liam Lane tastes like? I've thought about it in the shower, in the tub, baking and doing my business accounting, watering my plants, and in bed at night. Sure, I had to sleep on my stomach for three days because of the welts on my ass, but it was worth it. Thankfully, I have a job that requires standing. I would never have made it as an office worker in a chair this past week. Each time I rub lotion over my ass, I think about him and the exquisite pain.

At the end of the day, he's a literal pain in my ass.

"When do you see him again?" Kailee asks, pulling me out of my daydream about how Liam's hand felt on the back of my neck. Warm. Safe.

I shrug. "Probably the next time he wants to complain about my job or issue me a fine."

I haven't seen him since he walked out of my house. Luckily, I have a busy week with two events. We're currently sitting in a suburban driveway at an adult birthday party and pumping out cookies like they're gold bars. We pulled into the driveway and made damn sure there wasn't even a tenth of an inch hanging in the street just in case Liam dares stop by and wants a new nickname.

Kailee takes another batch of brownies out of the oven, and we move around the truck, Liam forgotten. More customers from up the block come by, and I giggle that they're not even invited to their neighbor's party. We get a lot of that. Word gets around suburban neighborhoods fast when an edible truck is parked nearby. Sometimes, I even have Kailee post on Nextdoor sites in the area. Whatever we make for the party guests, we quadruple it for the neighborhood. Hence, we're baking another batch of everything and still have two hours to go at this house.

Kailee takes a payment at the window and then sucks in her breath, gasping like she can't breathe or is sucking her teeth through a straw. "Lorelei! He's here."

"Who?" I ask, already knowing the answer. A mixture of dread and excitement moves from my stomach to my chest while something else moves down to my lady bits.

I stalk to the window in time to see Liam shut his car door, peruse the front yard of the party with disdain, and flick his eyes to mine. Our eyes meet, and my shoulders slump. He can't find anything wrong with me being here, right? The truck is all the way in the driveway, the packaging is up to legal code, and I give my truck a quick glance to make sure it could pass a surprise health inspection.

His badge is at his waist, and a few party guests eye it and back away from him as he walks directly toward my truck. "Hey, Officer Hot Guy," one woman calls, holding a beer can in the air. "Look at us drinking and eating pot brownies right in front of you. You can't do a goddamn thing, can you?"

Liam ignores the woman and doesn't break eye contact with me. He doesn't even glance at Kailee or nod at her in greeting when he approaches the truck.

I pat my hair, mentally chastising myself for not doing more than throwing it into a quick side braid this morning. My black tank top has flour spots across my chest, and I'm a hundred percent certain I smell like a banana.

"Hi, Officer Butt Cream. Want a cookie?" Kailee asks, and I close my eyes with embarrassment. Why did I tell her?

Liam tilts his head to the side, his nose scrunches, and he finally looks at Kailee and then back to me. "You told her?"

I clear my throat. "If I call Chase right now, he won't know anything about it, right?"

Liam blinks twice and puts his hands on his hips. He looks down at my tires, and I cross my fingers that there's not some tire pressure code for food trucks that I don't know. I don't need another fine or another impending court appearance. I don't know how I'll face Liam in court for the first admonishment.

He doesn't speak, and I know that Chase knows. In fact, Liam doesn't meet my eyes, even though he couldn't take his eyes off me while he walked to the truck. "Can I help you, Officer Lane?"

He squints. Maybe using his official name instead of Liam was a bad idea. "Officer Lane? I think you can call me Liam."

"You should totally be on a first-name basis with someone that spanks you with a belt," Kailee chimes in.

I turn to her slowly, my eyes wide. "Don't you have somewhere else to be? Somewhere far away?" I ask through gritted teeth, jerking my head to the back of the truck. "Somewhere with headphones or earplugs? Maybe a gag or some duct tape?"

"Not far away, but I will go to the back of the truck and pull the bread out." She turns to Liam. "I take it you don't want to try Lorelei's banana bread."

Liam shakes his head, still speechless after the spanking comment. When Kailee walks away, he nails me with a wounded look. "You told her I spanked you?"

"I had to explain why I couldn't sit down for a few days. We had drinks. I couldn't sit on the bar stool."

He rubs the back of his neck, and I wonder if his hand feels as good on the back of his own neck as it did on the back of mine. My breath catches just as a customer comes to the window and asks for a cookie.

I process the payment and hand the cookie to the customer, careful to obey every rule and check the person's ID, scan it, and explain they cannot drive after eating it. Liam's eyes are on my face the entire transaction, and his ears are trained on every word.

"Why are you here?" I ask as soon as the customer leaves. "Am I in trouble again? If so, can I be punished in that fun way you do?"

"I'm sorry I hurt you."

I back away from the window where I was leaning forward, halfway hoping he was here to spank me again. With his hand this time. "Excuse me?"

"I'm sorry you couldn't sit down. That wasn't my intention. I thought it was sexy, and you had those books. I thought it would be a good time, and I really wanted to spank you. Hell, I really wanted to do a lot of things with you," he babbles. I should stop him, but this is damn interesting. I spread my hands on my counter and look down at him, watching as he fights the emotions on his face but can't control his mouth. "Your ass was so perfect, and you handed it to me on a platter, and I...oh, hello." His eyes flick to a tall, curly-haired woman suddenly standing next to him, slowly eating one of my cookies.

He quickly looks away when she smiles at him. "Keep going. I want to hear this," the woman says. "You can spank my ass if you're just going around spanking people."

Before I can open my mouth to speak, Liam turns to the woman, puts his hands on his hips, and smiles. "I'm only interested in her ass," Liam says, pointing to me as Kailee snorts from somewhere in the back of the truck.

The woman shrugs. "You're hot. You could do a lot of damage to my ass. I live over there if you change your mind and ever want to tear it up," she says, pointing to the house across the street.

She walks away, and Liam turns back to me, pinching the bridge of his nose. "I'm fucking this up, aren't I?"

"I'll ask one more time. Why are you here?"

"Will you go out with me?"

I was not expecting that. A fine, yes. Another ride downtown to the police station, sure. "What the hell?" My face is hot, and my armpits are suddenly wet.

He blows out a deep breath like he can't believe I'm making him say it again. "I would like to take you on a date, Lorelei."

"What kind of date?"

He looks up at me, meeting my eyes for the first time since he got out of the car. The intensity of his eyes makes me tremble. My hands inch toward the edge of the window like they're hopeful he'll hold them. "I want to take you out to eat and get to know you. No pot questions. No discussion of what you do for a living. Hell, I don't want to talk about what I do for a living. I just want to go out with you, buy you dinner, and maybe learn your favorite color or what kind of music you like."

I bite my lip and tap my foot, thinking. After a few moments of silence, he looks down at the ground like a chastised child that knows he's in trouble. He should be in trouble. He's tried to ruin my business or harass me more than once. I should tell him to fuck straight off and give him the middle finger as he drives away.

But I really want to go out with him.

Is it curiosity? Maybe. Is it my own special blend of masochism? I can't rule that out. But I also can't discount the fact that I want to know his favorite color and what kind of music he listens to. I want to know his brand of toothpaste and why he smells the way he does. Is it his soap? His laundry detergent? I suddenly need to know his streaming TV of choice and if he likes butter on his popcorn when he goes to a movie. I want to know if he prefers wool or cotton socks, and I yearn to know his sheet thread count so I can imagine how they'd feel on my skin.

"I get to decide what we do," I say.

Liam lifts his head and blinks like he wasn't expecting me to agree to a date with him. "You'll go out with me?"

"Yes, but I decide where to go. I don't want you to decide with your grumpy attitude. From what I know about you, I don't want to end up doing grave rubbings at a cemetery or watching a documentary at the university."

"What's wrong with documentaries?"

"I knew it," I whisper under my breath.

He waves his hands in front of his face. "Fine. What are we doing when we go out? That way, I'll dress appropriately."

"Wear something you won't mind getting butter on or ripping," I say. "And make sure to wear thick socks."

"Holy shit, where are we going?"

"To Crab House to hammer the shit out of crab meat. Don't worry, they'll give you a plastic bib and gloves. I also love hushpuppies more than life itself, but only if we get a side of tartar sauce with them. They're dead to me if there's no tartar sauce. After that, we're going roller skating."

"Roller skating?"

"Sure, they have adult nights. You're going to hold my hand during the couple skate and then you'll buy me a slushy before you let me win at Skee-ball. They have Skee-ball machines there. Then, you'll give me your Skee-ball tickets so I can buy a little stuffed animal and a mini pack of Skittles from the prize counter. Do we understand each other?"

"Right," he drawls. "Roller skating and crab bibs."

"You forgot the Skee-ball."

He takes his phone out of his pants pocket, unlocks it, and hands it to me. "Put your number in so I can text to set up this Skee-ball shit show."

"You've never played?" I ask, typing my number in.

He takes his phone when I hand it back and turns to leave. "What about me would ever make you think I've played Skee-ball, Lorelei?" His mouth turns up at the corners into an almost, dare I say it, smile. "I'll text you tomorrow."

He walks away, and I can't help but think about how often I've heard a guy say he'd text me tomorrow.

Chapter 15

LIAM

I can do this. I can do this. It's not a big deal. I've been on a million dates. Well, not a million, but I've done this a few times. It's just another date. I've dated since high school, and I'm an experienced hand.

Why does it feel like a big deal, then?

Maybe it's because this is the first woman I've gone on a date with where I've seen her in handcuffs *before* the date. A chuckle rises in my throat and catches there. Fuck, I'm a moron. I wish I could go back in a time machine and tell myself not to give her the first fine. Then again, if I hadn't fined her, I wouldn't have had her in my squad car and wouldn't know her for the goddess she is.

This is a stupid idea. I hope Lorelei isn't looking through her blinds right now because she'll see me scuffing my shoes on her front sidewalk and looking at her purple flowers lining the walkway. I don't know what she'll think, but I don't want her to wonder if the big, strong cop is scared to death to ring her doorbell.

Because the big, strong cop is terrified of ringing her doorbell.

What if this date is horrible? Even scarier, what if it's wonderful? I have to go to court for her fine next week and face her. It's ludicrous that I could finally back her up against the wall tonight and run my tongue over her lips and then face her in front of a judge next week to talk about the bad thing she did to get a fine.

I run my hands through my hair and breathe out as I walk to the door. I imagine Chase laughing at me for not ringing a woman's doorbell, and that makes my feet move. She opens the door as I raise my hand to punch the doorbell. Only then do I notice she installed a camera doorbell. Fuck. She's been watching me the whole time, and she has the receipts.

"Do you want to cancel?" she asks as she opens the door with a hurt look. "Because you seem pretty hesitant to even come to the door."

Giving her a look up and down the length of her body, there is no way I'm canceling this date. No man would cancel with those legs in tight jeans and a black knit shirt that fits every curve of her breasts. She must be wearing a pushup bra because I could reach out and palm those perfect breasts if I was a man without control. Simple Converse rounds out the outfit, and I've always been a sucker for a woman in Converse. As it is, my control wavers along with my hands, and I shove them in my pockets so I don't act inappropriately with her.

"Liam?"

Her voice pulls me out of thoughts of nuzzling those breasts with my stubble, and I blink twice. "I want to go. I'm just nervous."

She tilts her head. "You're nervous about going out with me? Jesus, Liam, you've been a dickhead to me and have both fined me and taken me to the station in your squad car. I think I have the priority on being nervous about going out with *you*. I may find myself in an orange jumpsuit."

From the back of the house, Bogey runs toward me, bringing a purple squeaky bone and dropping it at my feet. Thankful for the interruption, I bend down and stroke his fur. "Not right now, buddy. I'm taking your mom on a date so I can impress her enough to borrow you for park outings."

"Is that what you're using me for? To hang out with my dog?"

I straighten and smile, still keeping my hand on Bogey's head. He sits and lets me ruffle his floppy ears, and my heart fills with overwhelming love for this dog.

At least, I hope it's for the dog.

"Of course, that's why I'm here," I smile, trying to lighten the awkwardness between us. "Why did you think I was here?"

"For the kitchen counter action," she deadpans without shame, and my face suddenly feels hot. "I thought you wanted a repeat."

I clear my throat as Lorelei reaches behind her and grabs her purse, slinging the strap across her body. She puts Bogey in his kennel as my brain works through if it wants a repeat of the kitchen incident. When she comes back, I take a deep breath. "No kitchen action tonight. Tonight, you'll get a perfect gentleman," I say, gesturing to my car.

As the door slams behind her, I swear I hear a curse of what sounds like disappointment under her breath.

"Line it up real nice and then hammer the shit out of it, Liam," Lorelei gasps, blowing a lock of her hair out her face with a huff.

"I feel like I'm hurting it."

"You can't hurt it. Pound it, for fuck's sake."

We look at the steamed crab on the mat in front of me, and Lorelei sighs as she dips another hushpuppy into a small dish of tartar sauce. "Shit, Liam, it's dead. Hammer it."

I bring the crab mallet down onto the crab shell and grimace while I do it. I've never hammered crab before, and I'm not sure I'm doing it right. Across from me, Lorelei hums and shakes her shoulders as she makes an utter mess of our table.

I've always been a neat and clean eater, but it seems impossible to be neat and clean when you have to hammer your food to get to it. Napkins are strewn across our table and covered in butter. We're both wearing rubber gloves as we pull crab legs apart and separate the outer shell from various sea animals. Chewed corncobs are on a plate in the center of the table next to a bucket full of crab shell pieces and shrimp tails. I guess we had the same idea about eating our corn first and getting to the hard stuff last. I've already been through two bibs, and one of them fluttered to the floor, never to be retrieved.

"We look like toddlers," I say, picking through the crab shell for pieces of meat. "I keep expecting my mother to suddenly appear with a new bib and wipe the table off."

Lorelei shrugs. "They're used to it." She holds up her butter-coated gloves. "They've probably seen worse. But it's good, huh?"

I nod because she's right. The food is perfectly steamed, and the crab legs are pulling apart without much work. I had a hushpuppy for the first time since childhood, and I can see why she likes them so much.

We work on our food in silence for a few seconds. For someone that was desperate to take her out and spend time with her, I can't think of anything to say.

Lorelei wipes a spot of butter off her outer lip and stops with her hammer mid-air over a new crab. "How is your mom?"

My eyes flick to hers, and I almost lean over the table to kiss her. Nobody really asks about Mom. Chase does when he thinks about it, which isn't very often. Mom's had cancer for so long that people have gone numb to asking about it unless I bring it up. "She's weak. It's hard seeing her like that."

"Chemo?"

I nod. "She's at max for radiation, so that's not an option. The doctors say it's looking good for her to beat it since they found it fast. The chemo is awful this round, though."

She chews a piece of food and swallows, staring at me the whole time. I feel myself blush under her gaze. The woman can't even look at me without me acting like a lovesick fool.

"I bet people two hundred years from now will look at chemo and think we're ignorant barbarians. They'll probably laugh at it like we laugh at leeching," Lorelei says, oblivious to my unease.

"Let's hope they find something better. I'd be disappointed in science if they didn't."

"Is she taking anything for it?"

I look behind her, trying to remember the bottle on Mom's kitchen counter. "I think a steroid. She doesn't like it. She says she gets all this poison pumped into her, and the last thing she likes is taking more meds on top of it. She does what the doctor says, though."

"You get that from her then?"

"What do you mean?" I ask.

"You do everything anyone tells you."

I stop cracking a crab leg open mid-crack. "I do not."

"When was the last time you broke a rule or went against what you were told?"

I look out the window next to me, squinting like I'm trying to see out into the night. "Well..." My voice fades. When *was* the last time I did something I wasn't supposed to do?

"You can't even think of one."

"I can."

She shakes her head and smiles. "It's fine, Liam. It's who you are." She makes a blade with her hand and holds it in front of her. "You follow a straight line. No going off course. No trying a different road. It's you, and I guess people need to understand that if they want to be in your life, right?"

I nod and inhale. Here goes nothing. "Do you, uh, want to be in my life?"

Her eyes widen. "This is just a first date, right?"

"I'm just wondering if you want to hang out more."

She looks down at her food, and my heart drops to my feet. Please say yes. Please say yes. Does she need a love letter? I'll write one. Does she need morning texts to remind her that I'm thinking of her? I'll send them. I just want to be around her more. It enrages me that I want to be around a drug seller, but I can't fight it any longer. I have no energy left to fight her freckles or those breasts. I can't argue with that voice any longer without also wanting to hear it hum around my dick. No heterosexual man could fight that ass.

"Liam, you've made it clear you hate what I do for a living. I'm not giving up my business. I love it. Other people love it. I'm starting to make decent money and pay back my small business loan. By the end of the year, I'm forecasting to buy another truck."

I squint. "A second drug den?"

She laughs and cracks open crab legs a little harder than necessary, staring at me. "Jesus, Liam, it's not an opium tent. Can you quit your job and run it for me?"

"Absolutely not."

"Why do you hate my job so much? You obviously like me. I know you do. I felt your cock on my butthole. Are you really that turned off by my job?"

"Yes," I say, pounding the table. She startles, and I shake my head. "I'm sorry. I don't mean to sound so angry, Lorelei. I just hate it. You could be so much more."

"Let me ask you a question." She furrows her brow and tilts her head. "If I was a nice little pie baker with my cute little apron and pleasant disposition, where would we be right now?"

I pause my mallet. Even my heart stops. Every muscle in my body wants to look away from her, but I won't. I refuse to look away from her challenging eyes, boring into me from across the table. "We'd be in my bed with your panties bunched on the floor, and you'd already have a ring on your finger."

It comes out, and I suddenly realize it's honest. Never have I been so obsessed over a woman. I want to know what she's thinking. I wonder what she's wearing every day I don't see her. Yesterday, I went shopping and searched for her soap again. Fine, I've done that more than once now. It's a selfish store run because I want to wash my dick with it.

God damn me to hell, but I've imagined her pregnant with my child, her breasts full and her belly rounded. It's a new image in my mind, only tempting me the last couple of days, but it's there. And it disturbs the shit out of me every time I think about it.

She's silent, chewing on something that isn't food, her tongue maybe. Her eyes flash angry, but there's something else there. The air crackles between our hands on the table, and I want to touch her, even wearing these stupid buttered gloves. Can I reach over and grab her hand? Can I hold a drug baker's hand in a crab restaurant?

I can't take it anymore. "Talk to me." More silence from her. Her leg shakes, and it jostles the table. "If you want to hit me for being a dick to you all those times, go ahead and hit me with your buttered plastic glove right here, Lorelei."

Her smile starts slow, and she tries to fight it. Her lips close together, her cheeks getting pinker until the strain is too much. She covers her mouth with a giggle, instantly getting butter all over her face. I reach for napkins from the dispenser and lean over the table, wiping the butter from her mouth and the tip of her nose.

"Are you giggling at the buttered glove slap idea?" I ask.

"Yes, I'm imagining slapping you with a buttered glove."

"If I wasn't a drug task force agent and you were a nice pie baker, where do you see us?" I ask, unable to help it. I want to know.

She stiffens and takes the napkins from me, suddenly growing serious. "I think I'm done eating and ready to kick your ass in Skee-ball now."

"Are we not going to talk about this?"

"Nope," she says, shaking her head and signaling for the waitress.

Chapter 16

LORELEI

"There's definitely a smell about this place," I mumble, running my sleeved arm over my face. I try to cover my nose without making it look like I'm covering my nose. "It's worth the smell of teen body odor embedded in the walls and skating rink food to kick your ass in Skee-ball."

Liam frowns as I shake my fistful of tickets in his face. "You cheat," he growls.

"You throw too hard. You have to have a gentle touch. It's all in the wrist."

He puts his hands on his hip and looks out at the skating rink where a few middle-aged couples are holding hands, trying to relive their youth. "I have a gentle touch."

"You weren't so gentle when you put your cuffs on me when you took me in."

He turns to me, and his forehead wrinkles like I hurt him. "Did I hurt you?" he asks, his voice husky.

I shrug and take a drink from the slush he bought me. He held up his end of the deal on buying the cherry flavor for me. "A little. I wouldn't classify you as gentle."

He smells good tonight. Like...*let me lick you to see if you taste like a pine forest* type of good. This infernal man has me doing mental whiplash. One minute he hates me for my job. The next minute he looks at me like I'm lunch and he's starving.

And what was up with that ring comment at dinner?

I put on a cool face, but that comment made me tingle right down to my toes. If he wasn't the guy that tried to ruin my business and is making me appear in court, he'd be my ideal guy. Tall. Gorgeous. Sexy. Good job. He's obviously alpha about protecting and providing for a woman. He wouldn't let me pay for dinner, not even my share, and he grabbed the ticket from the waitress before I could get a finger on it. He wouldn't even let me leave a tip.

I was totally joking about him having to buy me a slushy. I've always been a girl that could pay for my own dates. At the very least, I contributed with something like dessert or movie popcorn. The money coming in the last couple of weeks is more than I forecasted as word gets around about my truck.

This is a man that would take care of me if I let him.

"I'm sorry if I hurt you, Lorelei. I've never been trained to be super gentle when cuffing someone. Cuffing a criminal requires a firm grasp." He looks away and runs his hand down his scruffy face. Fuck, I love that scruff and wonder what it'd feel like on my inner thighs. Does he look a woman in the eye as he goes...

My thoughts trail away because he takes my hand. It's gentle and warm, and he slides his fingers between mine. I think my eyes even flutter a little. "I promise to be gentle from now on."

Yeah, I'm going to need him to fuck me hard if we ever get there, but I can't answer him because my mouth is cotton. His hand feels so damn right in mine. Even though his hand is substantially bigger and more masculine, a vein running up his tan hand into his chiseled forearms, I can't help but run my thumb over the top of his fingers. He inhales sharply and blows it out as he looks away.

"Well, since we're already holding hands, do you want to couple skate?" I ask.

He chuckles. "I haven't done this in something like fifteen years. What if I fall on my ass?"

"Then I'll laugh hysterically and take a picture for my Instagram. Hell, I may even go live."

"At least you're honest," he mumbles as I pull him along in his skates. He wobbles and reaches for the nearest wall. I'm not exactly a professional, so I'm grateful for the wall as I get my bearings.

I give him a few seconds and then silently pull him out to the rink, both of us taking baby steps in the skates. Like the gentleman he is, he lets me have the side closest to the wall, even though this was my idea. The disco ball turns over the rink, making little lights sparkle and trail over the path in front of us. His left arm is out, maintaining his balance, and a look of concentration is etched on his forehead. Thankfully, we both stay upright.

Nobody laughs or points as we circle the rink. Other couples our age or older sail by us, but we're certainly not the only people stumbling. Some even hug the wall, laughing as we go by them.

He holds my hand the whole way around as we circle the rink several times. After the third time around, we get our groove, speeding up a little. His body relaxes next to mine.

"My legs are going to hurt tomorrow," he says. "New activity and all. I lift, but I haven't used these muscles in a long time."

"Thanks for coming."

"Do you do this often? You seemed excited to come."

"No," I shrug. "I just wanted to see if you'd do it. You don't strike me as the crab restaurant and roller rink kind of guy. I'm actually surprised you played along."

"So, it was a test?" he asks, smiling. "Did I pass?"

"You passed."

We skate in silence for a few minutes. "Liam?" I ask, thinking about if I want to even ask my next question. He watches the floor in front of him but leans toward me a little. "What happens in court next week?"

"I don't know," he says with a grimace. "I know I'm going to have to go and face you, and I don't know how I'll face you in court when things have obviously changed between us since I took you to the station."

"Would you say you like me more now?" I ask, pasting on a debutante smile that he doesn't even notice.

"I know you better. I know you're not outright malicious like some drug dealers. I know you're beautiful, and I flat-out love your dog."

"I knew it. This is all a ruse to get to my dog."

He laughs a little, and I squeeze his hand harder. The pressure causes him to stumble, but he rights himself before falling and bringing me down with him. "Have you had enough?" I ask.

"Have you had enough? This is my test. Did I skate enough to earn a gold star?"

"I think you can take me back to my house now. I won't torture you any longer."

We stop at the nearest corner and hug the wall. Shimmers from the disco ball cross his face, and he turns my hand over, placing a kiss in the palm of my hand.

"Why did you do that?" I ask.

"I just wanted to kiss your hand, I guess. I've been holding it for the last twenty minutes."

"No, seriously. Why did you do that? We just played eight rounds of Skee-ball, and do you know where those balls have been?"

"Shit," he mumbles under his breath. "I can't do anything right when it comes to you."

I laugh and roll us over to the skate rental counter to get our shoes back. "You'll need to sanitize your mouth now, Liam. It's filthy."

"You have no idea."

When we pull into my driveway, I see Bogey at the window. He licks the glass and wags his tail at us as Liam insists on coming to my side of the car and opening the door for me. "Your protector is excited to see you."

"He's excited to see both of us. I've never seen him take so well to someone," I say. "You know he's the only reason I agreed to a date. Dogs can tell when people are good or bad. I guess you aren't so bad. It looks like he finagled his way out of the kennel, though."

"Can I walk you to the door?"

"Sure," I shrug, trying to be cool.

My stomach flutters, and a quick glance at Liam shows him flexing his jaw like he's chewing on his cheek. Why is this walk-to-the-door moment so awkward on every first date? It's been awkward since high school. Do I kiss him? Do I wait for him to kiss me? Do I want him to kiss me?

I totally want him to kiss me. If nothing else, I want to know what Liam Lane tastes like and how warm his mouth feels on mine. If it's a shitty kiss, I can remove all thoughts of him from my mind.

Please let it be a shitty kiss. I send a prayer up to whatever deity is in charge of my life. If he kisses me and it's bad, I won't think of it when I see him in court next week. I'll simply move on with my life and write Liam Lane off as a douchebag that tried to destroy my business but has a pretty face and a warm hand. I'll chalk the kitchen counter episode as a fluke and move on with my life, certain to never let another man spank me with a belt.

"I'll see you later, Lorelei. I had fun. I hope you did."

He's not going to kiss me. My stomach drops, and it's everything I can do to not let my face show disappointment. I overcompensate, giving a toothy grin and nodding as I fumble with my keys.

"Here, let me." He takes my keys from me and opens the door. "You have problems with keys."

"You're a distraction," I say as he moves away from me. Too far away.

"I'm the distraction? You have no idea, ma'am." He backs away a little, but he looks at my lips. "I'll see you later."

I nod. "Good night, Officer Lane."

"Good night, Ms. Rogers."

He turns and walks away, and I push my door open, breathing out a sigh of disappointment. Bogey greets me and wags his tail, but he also yips at something behind me. It takes a moment to realize my storm door is opening wider, and I turn around to find Liam an inch from me.

"Did you f-forget something?" I ask, my voice shaking.

"I sure fucking did," he says, cupping my cheek. Fuck, that hand is even warmer on my face than in my palm. "I forgot to do something I've wanted to do since the first time I saw your boob hang out that damn drug den window."

I don't sass him back or ask what he's talking about. I don't play coy because I've wanted to kiss this asshole since the first time he poked his head through my window and took my last damn cupcake.

He brings his lips to mine, and my knees turn weak. All hope that this guy doesn't know how to kiss a woman flies out the window as I wrap my arms around his neck. His lips move over mine, hungry but not rude. I open my lips a little, and his tongue respectfully searches my mouth. He hums a little at my taste, probably enjoying the remnants of cherry slush the same I'm enjoying the beer he had with dinner. His lips are warm against mine, but it's his body that sets me off.

I curl into his body like I'm butter melting into him. He lifts me a little since he's so tall, and I hold on to his neck for dear life before letting go and relaxing into his kiss, letting him hold me however he wants. I run my hands down his chest and feel every pectoral and every abdominal muscle as my hands finally rest against his belt. He whimpers a little when I stop there, and I feel him harden against my stomach.

I pull away, but he doesn't like that I break the kiss. He places tiny kisses against my lips, his eyes still closed and his forehead resting against mine. "Do you want to come inside?" I ask.

"No," he mumbles against my lips.

I shake my head a moment. Did I really get denied here? "No?"

"No, sweetheart. I want you to miss every inch of me tonight. Consider it my own test."

He kisses me on the forehead one last time and pries himself away from my body. His eyes are hooded, and if he isn't going to fuck me, he's going to go home and jerk his dick off to get our kiss out of his mind. Maybe he's fine with that. As for me, my poor vibrator has no idea what it's in for tonight.

"You're evil," I yell as he walks away from me.

"See you soon, Lorelei. One way or another," he calls over his shoulder as he gets into his car.

Chapter 17

LIAM

Fuck, it's been a few days, and I can't get her out of my mind. That kiss was epic, and I can't believe I had the discipline to walk away from her when she asked me inside. I took a long shower when I got home after the date, came twice, and watched my come circle the drain, only to wish I had come inside of her instead.

"Did you want some more spaghetti, Liam?" Mom asks, making me choke on the food in my mouth. I hope it wasn't obvious I wasn't listening to her as she rattled on about the minister that keeps coming by the house. Pardon me for not wanting to hear about a good-looking old minister that keeps sniffing around my mother. "You're a growing boy."

"I haven't grown in seventeen years, Mom."

"You'll always be my baby boy." Mom teeters over to the stove and dips another helping of spaghetti for herself.

I'd nag that she should let me serve her, but I'd only get shot down. I'm tiptoeing around her as it is since I'm trying not to upset her appetite. It's rare she eats, and she's eating tonight. "Thanks for dinner."

"Thanks for bringing my books by. I needed some new BDSM material."

"You and me both," I mumble, dropping my gaze to the remnants of roasted broccoli on my plate.

"What was that, dear?"

"Nothing. I said I'm glad to see you up and around."

"Have you seen that lovely girl you brought over a few weeks ago?" Mom asks, dropping the serving spoon in the pan. "I have enough spaghetti. I'll fix her up a container, and you can take it over to her. She seems like the type to return my good Tupperware."

"Jesus, Mom, don't do that."

"Why? Because you say she's a criminal?"

I growl like a bear, and it surprises me. I've never made that sound, especially not at something my mother said. What the hell is Lorelei doing to me? "I can't go over to her house tonight."

Mom sits back down in her seat and tilts her head, her eyes sparkling like I haven't seen in a long time. "Tonight? Have you gone over to the drug criminal's house before?"

From the look on my mother's face, she knows that I have. In a way, it's good to see Mom in a sassy mood. "I've seen her." I dip my head and shovel more food into my mouth.

"Did you finally collect your balls and go on a date with her?"

"Yeah," I mumble, still chewing. No use lying about it.

The silence is tense, and the only sound is the ticking of Mom's grandfather clock in the next room and the scrape of my fork against my plate. "Are you in love with her?" My mother asks, and I look up from my plate.

Mom stares at me with sad eyes that indicate she just wants her son to find love. I don't know why that someone has to be a woman that owns a pot van, but we can't always help who we fall for. Lord knows I fought it as valiantly as I could.

I look down again and ball my napkin in my hand, squeezing it. "Yes, ma'am. I think I am."

Mom claps her hands and holds her clasped fingers to her chest. "I knew it. There's something about that girl."

"Yes, Mom. I know there's something about her that people can't help liking. She may sell pot, but she's the human equivalent of crack."

Mom giggles and gets up from the table, slowly pushing away and rising from her seat. She shuffles over to the cabinet and grabs her old orange Tupperware bowl that once belonged to my grandmother.

"What are you doing? You can't seriously expect me to roll over to the drug pusher's house and offer up my mother's spaghetti as an apology for having her go to court tomorrow."

Mom spins around as fast as a recovering cancer patient still weak from chemo can spin. "You're actually going to show up?"

"Of course! It's my job to show up when there's a court case about a perp I took in."

"If the officer doesn't show up, doesn't it get thrown out?"

"I think that's only for traffic tickets, and it depends on the jurisdiction."

"Don't go to court. If you go, it'll ruin any chance you have with her."

"It's my job, Mom. Also, maybe it'll be the kick in the pants Lorelei needs to stop selling drugs out the back of a van."

Mom dips a huge portion of spaghetti into the Tupperware dish and scoops some roasted broccoli to the side of it. She gingerly lays a piece of garlic bread at the top of the container and burps the lid closed. Handing it to me, she raises an eyebrow. "Go take this to your lady friend."

"Now?"

"Now. Before you fuck up things beyond all repair tomorrow. You'll thank me later."

I doubt I'll thank my mother at all. I knock on Lorelei's door, not daring to hesitate this time, lest I be caught dawdling on the doorbell camera. Bogey yips at the door like he can smell me through the cracks, and Lorelei comes to the door, opening it in a pair of short pajama boy shorts and a Dolly Parton t-shirt. Her nipples show through the white of the t-shirt, and I look away. I can't handle seeing those nipples right now.

"Aren't you out late for a guy that has to face a menacing criminal in court tomorrow?"

I look at my watch and notice it's ten at night. "Shit. I didn't realize it was that late. I don't suppose you're hungry?" I say, holding up the Tupperware. "Mom made spaghetti and insisted I bring it to the nice lady I brought for her to meet."

"Do you do everything your mother tells you?"

"Yes. She's the only woman I'm scared of."

Lorelei smirks and crosses her arms, pushing those perfect tits up further. "Is that so? The only woman you're afraid of, huh?"

Maybe not the only one. I'm afraid Lorelei will never talk to me again after tomorrow, even if I don't want to admit it. I'm also afraid I'll never get my hands on those breasts.

"I'll go," I say, jerking my neck toward my car parked in Lorelei's driveway.

"Do you want to come in for a few minutes? I was just finishing up my baking for tomorrow. I had to get it done early because some douche nozzle is taking my time up tomorrow morning by making me appear in court."

I'm in the door and in her entryway before I can think about the consequences. Lorelei takes the leftovers and walks to the kitchen as Bogey and I follow. His tail thumps against me as he walks beside me, and I pat his head the whole way there.

Lorelei's kitchen smells like banana bread, but it also has the unmistakable smell of weed. I wrinkle my nose, and she gestures to the slow cooker in the middle of the counter. A fan that sucks the smell to the outside runs loudly in the window frame above the slow cooker. "I'm infusing. Do you want something to drink?"

"No." I shake my head. I have no idea what to say to her now that I'm in her kitchen. Damn Mom and her ideas.

"You're not saying much. We're already awkward as fuck together. It's going to be awkward as fuck tomorrow. Why are you here? And don't give me that shit about your mom telling you to swing by. You could have eaten those tomorrow without bringing them to me, and she'd be none the wiser."

"I had a great time on our date a few days ago. Whatever happens tomorrow, Lorelei, I don't want it to ruin our friendship." It comes from my chest, and I don't take it back. I say it as confidently as I say my own name.

She laughs at me. The woman actually laughs and holds her stomach. "We're friends? Is that what we are now? Fuck, Liam, am I the only one with whiplash here?"

"No, you are certainly not."

"Do you even know how you feel about me? One minute you hate me and are lecturing me like I'm a fifth grader in the drug prevention program. Then you're taking me down to the station. The next minute you've got me against the counter with a belt. The minute after that you're laying a kiss on me like I've never felt before after having a sweet date!" She runs her hands through her hair. "You're going to tell a judge what a horrible person I am tomorrow. God damn you to hell. What the fuck do you want from me, Liam? What are you even thinking right now?"

Bogey backs away from her, his tail between his legs like he's being scolded for shitting on the rug. I take two steps forward, my nostrils flaring, and I can feel the heat in my face.

"Do you want to know what I think?"

"Just tell me what the fuck is going on, you cowardly mother fucker!"

I chuckle and ball my hands into fists. I'd never hit her, but the angry energy needs to go somewhere. "I should hate you, Lorelei. Everything in my body and past training tells me I should hate you for what you do and how you make your living." I inhale deeply, and I know I'm going to regret telling her the truth. Somehow, this will lead to guilt and misery. "But I can't hate you. I can't hate you because you do things to my head. Sick things and wonderful things. You do things to me I can't admit to myself."

"Are you fucking kidding me right now?"

"Stop! I'm not done. I'll tell you when I'm done!" I yell the words, and I hear how bossy they sound, but I need to get this out.

I step toward her, my index finger an inch from her face, and she steps back into the counter, her eyes wide. "Don't you ever think that I don't have feelings for you, Lorelei. I may not know what they are or even how to deal with my conflicting feelings, but they are there, and they will not go the fuck away, no matter how hard I've tried getting you out of my system."

Her chest heaves, and those damn tits move with it. I focus my eyes on her face, but they're in my peripheral vision, and my cock hardens against my pants. At this point, I don't even care if she sees it.

"Fuck you, you fucking bastard," she yells. I wait for the slap across my cheek, but it never comes.

Instead, she does something even worse than hitting me. I'd take a slap across the face instead of the way her eyes flash fire.

Heat.

Heat moves through me, and I know it moves through her as her face reddens right up to the tips of her ears. She moves closer to me, enough where she feels my erection against her stomach, and the little bitch writhes against it as she grips my t-shirt and pulls me down for a kiss.

We kiss with urgent anger. Maybe it's lust, but I'm pissed off. I'm pissed off that I'm utterly fucked over this woman. I'm pissed that I've become vulnerable with a woman that should be my sworn enemy.

At the end of the day, I'd take a bullet for her. Right here. Right now.

I cup her cheeks and move my lips against hers, tasting the banana bread mixture she must have sampled. Something tells me her mouth is just that sweet, though. I reach down and cup her ass cheeks, pulling her up until she snakes her legs around my waist, making me moan with the feel of those beautiful legs circling my body.

She pulls at my hair, moving my head back as she kisses across my throat. The feeling makes my knees weaken, and it's all I can do to keep us upright.

She pulls away and bites at my lip. She's rough and wild, and I'm full of a need I've never felt before. "Bed. Now. Go," she breathes out in a husky voice.

I turn and walk us down her hallway, my dick hard against my pants and yearning for her like it's never wanted anything before.

Chapter 18

Lorelei

My room is dim, with only my small nightlight lighting the way. Liam holds me as he kicks the door closed behind us to keep Bogey out. He'd probably jump on the bed and be curious about what his two favorite people are doing, so I'm glad Liam had the forethought to shut the door.

Then again, if the erection Liam's sporting is any clue, I don't think Liam's thinking of anything except sliding himself between my legs and staying there until dawn.

He lays me on the bed, and I keep my legs around him as he stands straight and takes his shirt off. I hiss as soon as his t-shirt hits the ground, and I bend up to run my hands down those muscles. I toy with the patch of light chest hair in the center of his chest, letting it idly slide through my fingers. "Fuck, you're smoking hot, Liam. Has anyone ever told you that?"

"Not anyone that mattered," he whispers, pulling my own t-shirt over my head since I'm in a sitting position.

He throws my shirt across the room, where it lands on my dresser. He pushes me back to the bed and gets on his knees.

Holy fuck, Liam Lane eats pussy.

He makes short work of my shorts, and I wipe my hair back from my face as I try to remember the last time I got a full wax. The thought that I may not be exceptionally beautiful in the downtown area makes me squeeze my thighs together as he holds my knees apart.

He looks up. "Spread those beautiful fucking thighs before I do it for you."

"I didn't wax."

"If a guy's going to eat a pussy, a guy wants it to taste, smell, and feel like a real pussy. If I wanted a perfectly bare slit with no smell, I'd get a sex doll. Spread your fucking legs, Lorelei."

I blow out a breath and look up at the ceiling, embarrassed that I haven't had a good wax. Sure, he may *say* he likes it au natural, but it's probably just lip service.

Except it's not. His tongue slides up my slit, and he hums with approval as he buries his face. His tongue fucks my pussy as he tastes inside me, and his nose rubs against my clit as I grip his hair in surprise. He's not tentatively licking it. He's inhaling my very essence and savoring it like I'm that spaghetti he brought over earlier. I'm a meal to him.

His hair is soft in my hand, and I arch my back, bucking into his mouth. "Don't ever tell me you don't taste good or look good down here again, sweetheart," he murmurs. He looks at me when he says it, and I notice the wetness in his beard scruff.

Those brown eyes meet mine when I look down, and he holds the eye contact as he flattens his tongue and rolls it over my clit. It's my undoing.

Back and forth. Up and down. He moves his tongue over my center and looks at me, watching my expression the entire time. My core tightens, my legs over his shoulders tremble, and I release his hair, choosing to pull at my bedspread in a fit of uncontrollable pleasure instead of pawing at him. I don't want to moan for him. I don't want to give him the satisfaction of showing that he's the best oral sex I've ever had – and I may have experimented with my female roommate just one night in college.

Liam fucking Lane rocks my world, and I hate him for it. I hate myself for loving every slide of his tongue up my clit.

I break apart, and my feet shake against his back, flexing and pointing as I whine something that sounds like his name. I pull at my own hair, reach fruitlessly for my pillow like it's a life raft, and hate him for smiling into my orgasm. Because the bastard fucking smiles as I come all over his face, not stopping once. He eats my pussy through the orgasm and even gives it one last lick as soon as every tremble stops.

My body throbs for more as he stands, pushes me further up the bed, and undoes his belt. "Be gentle," I mutter, and I hate the begging in my voice.

He looks at me with angry eyes as he unzips his pants. "No," he sneers, his lip curling. It's such a simple word, but full of authority and dripping with innuendo. "I fuck hard, or I don't fuck."

Holy shit, I'm going to get fuuuccckkkeeed.

I lean up and kiss his chest, and he throws his head back as his fingers curl in my hair. "I've wanted this for so long, Lorelei."

"How long? Tell me," I taunt.

"Since I saw you. I had to have you. I couldn't stay away because I wanted this right here," he whispers, sliding his middle finger inside me.

I slide my hands down his chest and look up at him. He's already a wreck. Wetness glistens in his stubble, and his hair already looks like he's fucked a team of hookers. His cheeks are pink in the dim light, and his chest moves as he pants. His hands slide into his pants as he touches himself, and I can't help it any longer, I slide his jeans down his hips and look down.

"Holy shit," I gasp. "I have to tell Kailee you need a new nickname."

"No more Officer Half Inch?" he laughs. "I was starting to get used to her coming up with a new lewd nickname for me every time she saw me."

I glance down at him again, and my mouth waters. His dick is red, weeping with want, and it's fucking huge. "I think we'll have to go with Officer Energy Drink Can from now on."

He brings his hands to my hair, winding his fingers through the already tangled mess. He leans down to kiss me and pushes me back against my mattress as he wriggles out of his pants. Electric energy pings every spot his hands touch as he roams them over my body. He touches my neck, my arms, and my breasts, even bending down and licking them as if to say hello before he kisses my lips. I taste myself on him, and he nudges my legs further apart.

His thick form is on top of me, and his cock is at my entrance. I know I can take that monster dick, but fear suddenly grips me. There's no turning back from fucking him. I tremble, and he stops. "Are you scared of me?"

"No, I'm just scared of consequences, Liam."

"Do you want me to use a condom?" he asks, misunderstanding.

"I have an IUD. I just don't want you to think this lets you off the hook with anything."

He smiles an evil smile and slides into me slowly, his eyes fluttering and his mouth opening before he sighs. "Wouldn't dream of it."

The fullness is electrifying as he swivels his hips, and he buries his face in my neck, giving my jaw a small kiss. "How long have you wanted this, Lorelei? Tell me."

"Since I-I s-saw you, Liam."

He pulls out and thrusts into me hard, and I arch my back into him. My legs and arms wrap around his warm skin, and my fingers trail the muscles of his back as he thrusts into me over and over, sighing and saying my name every few thrusts. He curses, kisses my jaw, and props himself on his elbows as I kiss every inch of him I can reach. I kiss his throat, his jaw, and his chest when he throws his head back.

My headboard bangs against the wall with his thrusts, and I'll feel him tomorrow. Maybe I'll even be sore from his cock when he looks at me across the courtroom. Will he think of me like this then? Will he flash to me under him and moaning his name against his shoulder?

He suddenly pulls out and turns my hips, pushing me onto my stomach. I get the gist of his movement and get on all fours, unabashedly shaking my ass at him while he grips my hips and shoves himself into me from behind. "Can I tell you a secret?" he whispers, smiling as he turns my face so I'm looking at him over my shoulder.

"Always."

"This is my favorite way to fuck."

"Good to know," I whimper, bucking back at him.

He takes his hands off my hips and stays still as I push back against him. "That's it, Lorelei. Go on and fuck me hard. Take what you want." He playfully slaps my ass again, and it only escalates my delicious frenzy.

I whimper and whine at the fullness and the sound of his thighs meeting the back of mine. When he finally grips my waist and joins in, I practically go through the headboard. He puts a hand up on the wood to brace us, and I bite my pillow.

He hammers the fuck out of my pussy, and I bite and drool on the fabric below me. I take every inch he gives me, and I'm powerless with his strong hands holding me in place. Eventually, he speeds up, and his thighs tremble, his body primed for orgasm. Only then do I realize how much I want to be the one that makes him come harder than he ever has.

I squeeze him, flexing my muscles around his length, and he moans. It's guttural and comes from his soul as every part of him shakes. His voice even trembles when he says my name one last time before collapsing in a heap on top of me, his hand idly stroking my cheek.

Chapter 19

LIAM

"Hey," I whisper, my eyes still protectively closed against the light coming through the blinds. "Good morning."

She's curled into me. Her back is warm against my stomach and chest, and that sweet-smelling hair tickles my face. It's been tickling my face all night, but I don't dare sweep it away. I want to keep it on my face as long as possible until we have to get up and face each other in court. Dread sinks into my stomach, but I can't decide if it's dread of making her feel bad about herself in court or dread that I have to leave her bed in a few minutes.

Maybe both.

She stirs beside me, and I tighten my arm that's thrown over her side. Kissing the back of her neck, I inhale deeply as her hand reaches back and strokes my morning scruff as if surprised to find a man in her bed.

Please don't let her regret last night. I can't bear it.

"I need a shower," she mumbles. "Some guy got me all messy."

I chuckle and smile into her shoulder and playfully bite it, tasting the salt of her skin.

And I did get her messy. I fucked her again before we finally fell asleep with our legs tangled. She snores, but I made sure she fell asleep first so I could watch her sleep for a few minutes. That may sound creepy, but I prefer to think of it as a protective instinct.

I reach between her thighs, stroking her gently and finding stickiness there. "You don't need to shower. You could just show up to court with my come still running down your legs, and I could look across the table from you and smile."

She pushes me away. "You're positively lewd, Liam Lane." She sits up, pulls the sheet over her tits, and looks like a work of art. The way she sits in the sun as the dust motes float around her makes me want to pull her back into bed, pull the sheets up, and kiss every inch of her, sticky thighs or not. "Want to hop through the shower with me? We could share water. It could be your good deed for the day."

She's already to her shower when I swing my legs out of bed and pad to the bathroom completely naked. I've dreamed about showering with her, and this seems surreal. In fact, I half expect to wake up in my lonely bed without her like last night was a figment of my imagination.

The steam fills the bathroom quickly, and we both duck into the shower, rinsing ourselves under the hot water. I slink an arm around her, and she shampoos my hair as I kiss her. Electricity moves through my body as she lathers my hair and the suds roll down my back. I don't break the kiss, but I lean over to grab shampoo and start washing her hair for her, dragging my fingers through the long hair to detangle it.

Her eyes close for most of the shower, luxuriating in the hair wash and my hands moving soap around her body, up her legs, up her stomach, over those perfect breasts, and even between her butt cheeks.

I give her butthole a jaunty little touch with my index finger, and she bites my chest.

Fuck, I'm going to be late for work, but I don't care.

But she can't be late today. I could not show up and nobody would care. If she doesn't show up to court, a warrant goes out. "We need to get you to court," I mumble as she lathers soap in her hands and starts to wash me.

Unfortunately, she also drags her hand over my dick a moment later, and I lose all sense of reason. "OK, Liam. This has to get clean first, though. I got it all kinds of dirty last night, didn't I?" she taunts.

"Fuck yeah, you did. It's all kinds of filthy. Better get the balls. They got dirty."

"I came so hard on you. No telling what's on this monster dick." She looks down at me and licks her lips. My hands grab the soap dispenser on the wall because I know where this dirty little bitch is going, and I don't want to fall down in pleasure. "In fact, I think I need to make sure it's extra clean. It could use a good spit shine."

I don't answer her taunt. I lean my head back on the cold tile that's in contrast to the hot water beating down my chest and grip her wet hair in a ponytail as she slides down my body. "Lorelei," is all I can whisper.

"Someone needs an unholy trinity."

I raise my head and look down at her. Fuck, there are those sexy doe eyes looking up at me. The eyes every man wants on them while they get their dick sucked. "What's an unholy trinity?"

She smiles an evil smile that reminds me how bad this girl is for civilized society and takes a long lick up my cock, humming in approval the whole way. "Well," she starts. She sucks the tip of my dick and pulls hard, flicking her tongue over the hole at the same time. "You'd think it would have something to do with me sucking your dick."

"Yes, ma'am. I'd like that, please."

"But I'm not going to do that."

"What?" I ask, suddenly terrified I've been hoodwinked and will have to walk into work with this monster stiffy.

"I'm going to lick it clean. Then, I'll just jerk it. Those are the first two parts. I'm going to jerk your dick while I suck on your balls and work on getting them clean."

"That's nice. More of that," I nod, panting. Shit, this woman is going to kill me.

"Don't you want to hear the third part?"

"The third part?"

"It's an unholy *trinity*, Liam. I'm going to do three things to set you on fire."

"Do I want to know?" I ask in a high-pitched voice that I haven't used since my balls dropped in seventh grade.

She drags her tongue up my dick one last time, grips my cock in one hand, and takes my left testicle into her mouth like it's a spoonful of mashed potatoes. She sucks on it and jerks me off, and I think I'm having a stroke. My arms stiffen, my heart pounds out of rhythm, and I can't speak.

Fuck, I'm having a stroke in a pot baker's shower. If I die here, the entire department will talk. Everyone will think I was on the take, and Chase will have to defend himself against...

I jump suddenly, yelping. "What the fuck?"

"Funny that you think it's fine to nuzzle my butthole, but you don't like it when I do it." Lorelei looks up at me, her eyelashes wet from the running water. Drops run down her smiling face, and she still works me with her hand, knowing just how to drive me fucking bonkers as she runs her soapy hand all the way from base to tip. "Fair is fair."

"My asshole is exit only."

"You may really like it. Come on, Liam. Just one finger."

"God, you're a drug pusher and a butthole pusher."

She laughs, and the water that was on her lips sputters to the drain. "A butthole pusher? Is this a highway rest area?"

"I can't think of an actual word for it, but you're evil. It's like the people that jump out from behind trees and offer innocent people drugs."

"Are you saying that I jumped out at you and asked, 'Hey baby, you want to try a finger in your butthole? Just once won't hurt.'"

I moan as she dips down and takes my right ball in her mouth. She sucks this one even harder, and I arch my back against the tile, my toes curling against the white linoleum. I grip her hair hard, fisting it again so I can at least look like I'm dominant, but her mouth and hand feel so good that I'm dough in her hand. I wriggle against the linoleum, look up to the ceiling, and let the evil pot baker slide her middle finger into my asshole.

God damn me to hell, but I even open my legs a little. "You filthy little bitch."

She hums against my ball before moving to the other side, which is good because it was getting lonely. Even in the hot water, her mouth is warmer on my balls, and when she's not touching or licking me, I feel cold. Her hand expertly works my cock.

And that finger...

I now know why people talk about the prostate like it's the epitome of sexual pleasure. The tip of her finger bumps against it once, and I whine like a hurt animal.

But I'm not hurt. Dear God, I'm not fucking hurt.

She startles a little when I whine. Thankfully, she figures out what she did and moves back to it while I make another sound I've never made before. Fuck, I don't even know where I am right now.

"Right there, Liam?" she coos. "Is that what my big, tough, mean police officer likes?"

"Fuck!" I moan, fisting her hair and concentrating only on not falling on my face or on her in the shower.

I'm done.

Lost.

Fucked.

Ruined.

Shattered.

Destroyed.

I'm fucking in love. If I can't have this woman in her entirety, I'm going to marry her middle finger.

I pitch forward and hold myself up on the other side of the shower stall as I curl into my orgasm. When my balls tighten around her tongue, she moves her mouth to the end of my cock and swallows every drop I give her.

"Lorelei, you're out of coffee!" I yell. It's not like she can hear me. She's showering alone now. Apparently, I'm too much of a distraction in there. I was kicked out, shirtless, to go make coffee before court starts in less than two hours.

I rummage around her cupboard and find green teabags, and I quickly fill up two mugs with water, stick the teabags in, and pop both mugs into the microwave as I busy myself with toast. At least she has bread and butter.

When the microwave and toaster go off at the same time, I butter the toast, humming to myself about the fantastic sex I've had in the last eight hours. I figured she'd be as much of a pistol in bed as she is outside of it, but last night and this morning with her was next level. I can't remember the last time I had so much fun in bed.

And the fucking feelings. I felt things I can't even admit to myself this morning.

I take the tea out of the microwave and steep the tea bags while I look for sugar. I know I saw a sugar bowl when I was here the night I took her to the station. Looking through the cabinets, I finally find it.

Empty.

How is a baker out of sugar? I can't have a cup of tea without sugar in it. I could, but it wouldn't be pleasant, and I don't have time to fuck around without a hot beverage this morning. I've never been able to drink straight tea.

I blow out a sigh and look around. She has to have some Splenda or Sweet 'n Low that'll do in a pinch.

I open the cabinet to the right of the sink and look around for small packets or even a large bag of bulk sugar. Every spice known to man is in here, and her cinnamon tumbles to the counter. She's a baker, so it makes sense to have every spice in existence, but it takes me a full minute to find the small bear container of honey in the back of the cabinet right behind where her large container of cinnamon was a moment ago.

I squeeze a small amount of honey into a spoon and give it a taste to make sure it's good. I don't think honey expires, but I'm not sure how long it's been at the back of the cabinet. I lick it, swirling the taste around on my tongue. It seems fine. There's a slight undertaste I can't place, but I squeeze more honey into a spoon, grab the mugs from the counter, and circle the spoon around my steaming cup of tea, leaving hers alone because I don't know if she drinks it straight.

The shower turns off, and I sip the hot liquid and nibble on toast, waiting for her to come into the kitchen so I can make her something else to drink if she doesn't want tea. I take my mug to the refrigerator and sip it while I peruse the contents of her fridge.

"Making yourself at home?" she asks, coming into the kitchen and giving me a wry smile. She looks down, and her shoulders slouch.

"Just looking through your fridge. My mother always said you can tell a lot about someone by their bathroom cabinets and their refrigerator contents."

She purses her lips and looks around the kitchen, not meeting my eyes. "Why are you being so shy?" I ask. "You weren't shy a few minutes ago with your finger up my butthole." I smile at her and wink over the mug as I raise it to my mouth and take a huge gulp. I have to go home and change, so I need to drink this fast.

She smiles again and takes the towel off her head. Shaking out her long hair, water drips onto the floor. "What should I wear to this court shitshow today? What would make me show my fining officer that I'm really an upstanding citizen?"

I walk to her and kiss her forehead. "If you want an arresting officer to think you're an upstanding citizen, you probably shouldn't finger the hell out of his prostate before court, sweetheart. Just a tip."

"It *was* just the tip," she mumbles, and I reach around and playfully slap her butt. She giggles and pulls away. "Are we going to talk to each other after this morning?"

"Do you mean after the unholy trinity or after court?" I ask.

"Court."

I take another big gulp of tea and look down at the mostly empty mug, swirling it and wishing I could drown myself in what's left of it instead of going to court. "I hope so. I hope you'll still talk to me when I call you tonight and ask you to dinner."

She playfully smacks my shoulder and smiles again until she sees the container of honey on the counter. She goes quiet, tilts her head to the side, and I can practically see the gears moving in her head as she blinks twice. I follow her eyes and shrug. "You're out of sugar. I hope it's fine that I looked through your cabinets and used the honey."

Her face is unreadable, and her expression moves from numb to hysterical in the course of a few seconds. She grabs my mug, notices the dregs at the bottom, and covers her mouth with one hand. Her expression is one of horror, even as her lips turn up at the corners. She backs away from me, wide-eyed and shaking her head.

"What? What's wrong. Is this rat poison or something?"

"Depends on what Officer Lane considers poison." She nods at the honey jar. "You ate infused honey, Liam. You're going to be as high as a kite in about an hour."

Chapter 20

LIAM

"Would you say I'm blinking more than usual?" I ask, looking into my phone on the selfie setting. "I think I'm blinking a lot. Can you tell? How many times a minute would you say I normally blink?"

Chase looks up from the Lambert file and frowns. The file is getting bigger, and we just about have enough to get a warrant. We know exactly who is coming and going and buying Lambert's product, so we're stacked with information for other suspects.

"Are you OK?" Chase asks.

I shrug. "Fine. Totally fine. Life is good, you know?"

"Did you get laid or something?"

I sputter a laugh. This stuff makes me want to laugh. At least, I want to laugh every few minutes. I feel like I'm riding a roller coaster of emotion. One minute, I'm calm and thoughtful. The next minute, I laugh and can't seem to stop. My Uber driver here was fucking hilarious. "Yep, sure did. I got laid out good, man. I even got my prostate tickled in the shower today. It's a beautiful morning!" I clap my hands, and Chase startles as my raucous laughter fills the bullpen. "I'm awesome! Hell, Lorelei is awesome. Everything is awesome." I point at him and try to look serious. "Are you awesome?"

He looks behind him and back at me. "Are you drunk?"

I wave my hands in front of us and knock over my pen cup. Pens skitter across the desk, and Chase catches one before it hits the floor. "No, I'm not drunk. I'm high as fuck. I accidentally ate her honey pot this morning, and I don't mean the one attached to her. She infuses her honey. How fucked up is that?"

"I think you should go home sick, man. You're in no shape for court today."

"Shh," I say, shushing Chase. "I'm just fine, but I have something important to ask you."

Chase leans closer like he expects me to ask him something about the Lambert file or work. He chomps the gum in his mouth, and I stare at his lips while they move. "Which do you think is scarier, Candyman or Bloody Mary?"

He sits back in his seat and sighs. "Candyman is way more terrifying."

"That's why I like you. You're honest. But what if you're listening to Lady Gaga's 'Bloody Mary' while you're looking in a mirror? Do you think she comes out?"

"Who? Lady Gaga?"

"Bloody Mary, you moron."

"Nah, man. You have to say it several times before she comes out of the mirror. Everyone knows that. I don't think Lady Gaga says it enough in that song."

"What if you listen to it twice in a row?" I ask.

Chase leans forward in his seat again, and I laugh at the squeaky sound of his department-issued chair. It's funny. He smiles and makes a *come here* motion with his finger. I lean forward and turn my ear toward him to hear better. "Dude, you sound fucking ridiculous. You are so fucked up, you're incapable of having an adult conversation." He jerks his finger over his shoulder in the direction of the courthouse next door. "If you go into that courtroom in fifteen minutes, you'll get us both fired."

"Why would you get fired?"

"You're going to fuck this up so royally, they'll fire anyone that knows you. Not only that, but you'll blow it with your girlfriend so bad you'll never get your prostate tickled again. Go home."

I swig my coffee from the station vending machine in the hopes it'll sober me up enough to function in court in fifteen minutes, but my hopes for that shatter when Chase grabs me by the shoulder a bit later and hauls me out of the chair. "Come on, or you'll be late, loverboy."

"Court doesn't start for fifteen minutes," I complain.

Chase taps my watch and smiles. "You've been staring at your coffee and swirling it in circles for literally fifteen minutes."

"Holy shit. Where did the time go? The colors in my cup were so pretty. The white of the cream blended into the black. It was mesmerizing."

"Walk." He grabs my arm and escorts me out of the building, walking me toward the courthouse as people passing by stare at us. It's not an everyday occurrence to see Chase marching his partner to the courthouse by the shoulder.

He escorts me to a small conference room and even walks me to the table where a court stenographer, the judge, and a representative from the district attorney's office sit. Lorelei and her attorney are already across the table, and I take a moment to admire Lorelei in a pink satin blouse with a little bow tied at the neck. I hold my hand out like I'm going to untie the bow, and Chase slaps my hand down.

Judge McNulty, an older woman with steel-gray hair known for her intolerance of bullshit, frowns. "Officer Lane, are you OK?"

"He's fine," Chase answers for me, slapping me on the back.

"Are you involved in this case, Officer Barnett?" Judge McNulty asks.

"Absolutely not. This is a complete waste of time and officer resources. Just delivering Officer Lane. He's a little out of sorts today, but he's physically fine. Have a nice day. Hi, Lorelei." He waves and smiles at Lorelei like they're old friends, and Lorelei ducks her head, looking away from him as her lawyer furrows her brow in confusion.

Lorelei ignores me, and I don't like that. I bob and weave my head in her line of sight, trying to catch her eye like an annoying teen boy, but I become aware that I probably look ridiculous bobbing and weaving. I put my head in my hands and focus on the wood grain of the table.

"Wood," I sputter, laughing at my thoughts about table wood from trees and the wood I was sporting this morning.

"What's that, Officer Lane?" Lorelei's lawyer asks, clearly smelling the stupidity wafting off me.

"Why do we call it wood?"

"Why is what called wood?" the judge asks.

It's clear this is going downhill fast, and I look at the wall behind Lorelei, focusing on not blinking. My hands flail a little because I don't know what to do with them. Somehow, it seems perverse to put them in my lap. The idea of touching myself at a court meeting suddenly strikes me as funny, and I laugh. I laugh so hard that my stomach curls, and I push my forehead to the table where I mutter incoherent words over and over.

Every eye is on me now, and nobody finds me as funny as I find myself. Only Lorelei looks at me with something akin to pity. She must feel guilty, and I hate that.

The rep from the district attorney's office leans over and taps me on the shoulder. "Are you drunk, Officer Lane?"

I straighten up, acting the picture of sober. "No, sir." I need to give an explanation for my behavior, though. I've always been the picture of professionalism in front of the district attorney reps and Judge McNulty. "I fear I have been drugged."

"Shit," Lorelei whispers across the table. She covers her eyes with her hands, and her attorney puts a hand on Lorelei's shoulder like she's in shock.

Only after Lorelei's curse do I realize I made a mistake. Lorelei's afraid that if I rat on her honey weed that she'll be in more trouble. It'll even look like she maliciously tried to sabotage the court hearing about her fine. I know she didn't do it on purpose.

Backpedal. Backpedal. Backpedal.

"Backpedal what?" Lorelei's attorney asks.

"Huh. I didn't realize I said that out loud. I thought it was in my head," I say, pointing at my temple.

Shit. What else have I said out loud? Please, God, don't let me have mentioned that I want to peel that soft-looking shirt off Lorelei's body and lick her from her toes to the tips of her ears right here on this conference table.

"When you say you've been drugged, are you talking about roofies?" Judge McNulty asks. "That's a serious accusation."

"Roofies would knock him out," Lorelei's lawyer says. "He seems pretty awake. Just ridiculous. It's like he accidentally ate the wrong type of brownie at a party."

Lorelei's face has panic written all over it, and the people around the table look at me like I'm a science experiment. The silence is deafening, and I clear my throat, straighten my shoulders back, and try to take my eyes away from the gorgeous woman across from me that I'd take a bullet for. "I'm fine. Let's get started."

"I think we should postpone this to another day," the district attorney rep says, closing Lorelei's file.

I can't do that to Lorelei. She's been nervous enough about this entire thing, and when I'm high, I see the ridiculousness of taking it this far with her. This is something she's worked hard for. Her business is on the line. Yeah, I want her to choose a different line of work, and I have no respect for what she does. I still think she is a bad influence on society.

I'd just rather cut off the testicle she had in her mouth this morning rather than hurt her.

"I want to get this over with today," I mumble into my armpit. I don't know why, but my voice sounds better from my armpit. Conference rooms have weird acoustics I've never noticed before.

"I've always had respect for you, Officer Lane, but I think this needs to be pushed to another day," Judge McNulty adds. "I know you wouldn't imbibe in drugs on purpose, so I'd like to discuss this with you when you're not high as a kite."

I shake my head and focus on sounding as professional as possible under the circumstances. My eyes droop, and I suddenly feel very tired. "I'd like this to be decided today. I insist we continue."

Lorelei's attorney types on her laptop and clears her throat. "Your honor, my client would like to get this over with. She wants to get back to her legitimate business. If Officer Lane can't control himself or his outbursts, we'd like to have this citation thrown out and struck from my client's record. Ms. Rogers has done nothing wrong, and we have competent statements from Buddy Wilkins that Ms. Rogers has permission to use the grounds." She emphasizes the word *competent* and nails me with a glare. "We're talking about a half inch of overlap onto a public walkway, and my client has drafted a formal apology to the court."

Judge McNulty sighs and looks over her reading glasses at Lorelei. "Ms. Rogers, I've never known Officer Lane to be petty, but even I'll admit that this is a petty fine and citation. Given the fact that Officer Lane insists on continuing with this today and has provided no other information on why I should pull your seller license, I'll grant your request to strike this from your record and nullify the fine." She points a bony finger at Lorelei, and the judge's face turns to stone. "If you do not follow the rules of this state to the letter of the law going forward, I'll not be so lenient if I see you in my court again. This is me telling you to stay out of my courtroom."

"Yes, ma'am," Lorelei says, and I smile at her like a love-sick schoolboy, even propping my hand on my chin and beaming at her. Lorelei sounds so professional, and I'm proud of her. This is my girl. Mine! Protectiveness moves through my chest. This woman had her legs around me just hours ago, and she's holding her own in court, even though her lawyer has done most of the talking.

"Case dismissed," the judge says, and Lorelei breathes a sigh of relief.

"On what grounds?" the district attorney rep asks, notating the file.

Judge McNulty looks at me over those reading glasses, and paranoia moves through my body like a brush fire. "Officer incompetence."

"I-Incompetence?" I stammer. Nobody has ever accused me of incompetence, even at my first job when I was fifteen.

"Don't take it personally, Officer Lane. You're incompetent today, but that doesn't mean you haven't been respectable your entire career.

You insisted on continuing today, and you were in no condition to continue. Have a nice day. Go home and sleep off whatever this is."

She rises, and everyone in the room stands up. After the judge leaves, everyone else packs up as I sit in the chair, stare at the wood grain, and don't even notice Lorelei leave. I stay in that room, losing all track of time and staring at the table until Chase comes to get me and drives me home.

Chapter 21

LORELEI

I shift the warm pan from my hand to my hip as I ring the doorbell. In the movement, the empty Tupperware dish on top of the pan almost tumbles to the ground with the plastic grocery bag full of books. Thankfully, Nola opens the door and catches the Tupperware before it hits the porch. The movement makes me smile. Her reflexes are still good.

"This is a surprise!" she says. Her voice is weak, but her smile is genuine. I stare at it a moment, thinking about how much her smile is like Liam's...when he actually smiles.

Looking closer at her, I notice little things about the resemblance between her and her son that I missed before. Her eyes are the same brown, her ears are dainty and close to her head like his, and I wish I could learn her hair color without seeming rude. I bet it's dark brown like Liam's when chemo hasn't taken it. As it is, she's rocking a floral headscarf that's stylishly knotted at the side of her neck.

I smile and hold the screen door open with my butt. "Hi, Nola. I wanted to stop by and return your Tupperware. I know how valuable it is with that lifetime warranty and everything. I also thought I'd save your son some trouble and go to the library for you." I wave the bag of paperbacks at her, and she gasps in joy, even clapping her hands.

"Oh, thank you. Liam doesn't read the description well, and I often end up with inspirational romance." She shivers like she has a chill, and I cringe. "Nothing wrong with holding hands, but I prefer a good dicking down. Come in! Come in and chat a bit. It's nice to see someone other than my son or the grouchy nurse the service sends over."

She waves me into her living room and immediately sits on her sofa, pulling a blue blanket over her legs. The effort to answer the door and shuffle around must have already zapped her energy. I sit across from her in the seat Liam sat in the last time I was here. Sinking into the soft fabric of the recliner, I wonder if this is his chair. Something about that makes me feel close to him.

I haven't seen him for four days. I texted him to see if he was alright after being high at court, and he responded he was. I haven't heard from him since, and part of me being at his mother's house is me returning the Tupperware.

Part of it is me fishing for information.

"How are you, Lorelei? Tell me everything."

"Well, I accidentally got your son high when he ate the honey in my cabinet, he made an ass of himself in court, and I haven't heard from him. I was kind of hoping he's told you his plans to never speak to me again because I sure wish he'd talk to me."

She laughs and rummages through the bag of books I brought her, nodding in approval as she pulls every book out of the bag, smiles at the cover, and stacks it next to others. "Quite the contrary. I talked to him briefly last night when he brought over a few groceries. He's busy at work. They're getting ready for some kind of big bust, and the only person he's been seeing is that smoking hot partner of his. I wouldn't mind if that Chase fellow came over and cheered up an old woman..." Her voice trails off, and I clear my throat. "Liam couldn't drive me to chemo the other day because he was filing paperwork to the judge."

I breathe out a sigh of relief that Liam not talking to me isn't about me this time. Lola notices my relief and tilts her head to the side. "You're falling in love with my son, aren't you?"

"If I am, are you going to tell him?"

"I'd never give him the satisfaction, honey." She slaps her legs and leans back. "If you're running as a wife candidate, you have my vote."

"Is that because he doesn't get out much?"

She shakes her head. "No. It's because there's been a change in him the last few weeks."

"What kind of change?"

"That stick that's been in his ass his whole life has started to wedge itself out a little. He doesn't stomp as much when he walks. It's like there's a kitten with glitter on his shoulder, and I think you're the glitter kitten. Has he told you he's falling hard for you yet?"

I fiddle with the aluminum foil on the pan of baked goods I brought her. "Do you think he's falling for me?"

"He hasn't said he is," she says, and my shoulders slouch in disappointment. No use hiding it from his mom. "But I know. I see something there. I saw it when he had you in handcuffs in my living room the first time. He's softer with you, and Liam has never been soft." She looks at the pictures on a side table, and I notice a picture of a boy of about thirteen with a mop haircut and braces. I never noticed it before, probably thinking it was a nephew. It's so...un-Liam. The kid is smiling like he's actually happy.

Nola smiles at the picture. "He was a happy kid. Don't get me wrong, he was a tough little bastard that didn't tolerate bullying. But happy. He didn't get hard *and* sad until Amanda died. That fucked him up bad. Then you popped up last month. Something is different. That's all I know."

Silence stretches between us, and I get up and fiddle with things on her coffee table, putting them into stacks. She watches me, probably glad for the help to tidy up a bit. I straighten her crochet project, and I take two empty bottles of water to the kitchen recycling bin. When I come back, Nola's in the same spot and watching me. Waiting for something.

I sit down in Liam's chair again and pat my braid. "I think I'm falling in love with your son. I just can't help it. There is nothing more fulfilling than getting that sour asshole to smile or laugh. Sure, I want to punch him in the throat about half the time, but that other half is destroying me."

She smiles. "I know, honey. I'm glad you love him. I think he loves you. Maybe you two should just forget about your differences, elope, and give me ten grandchildren."

I smile at the thought of having children with Liam, and Nola mumbles something under her breath I can't hear. What do you say to the mother of the man you love when you want him to love you back? Do I ask her to put in a good word with him?

I settle for more practical small talk. "How are you feeling these days?"

"Awful. Chemo's kicking my ass the longer it goes on."

"Liam says it looks good this time."

She nods. "It does. They just want me to finish the treatment to be sure they got it all with surgery and all the poison they've pumped into me. Some days, I can hardly move. The nausea is the worst. I have my good days when I'm able to keep food down and actually have an appetite, but those days are few and far between."

I look at the pan of brownies I brought her. "I may have brought you a present that isn't dick books. You can't tell your son, though."

"Oh, a secret?" Nola smiles, sitting up a little straighter.

"I made you some special brownies. You know what I mean." I wink at her.

"The kind my son would never approve of and has spent his career fighting?"

"Yes, ma'am." I pull the foil back and show them to her. "I didn't put nuts in them because I didn't know if you're allergic, and I didn't think about your lack of appetite. But if you feel like eating, eat one in the morning and one in the evening around dinner so you have an appetite. Small pieces. Not big ones unless it's not helping. Then go bigger. Oh, and don't let your son accidentally eat them, especially not before work or a court appearance. He certainly doesn't need these before sitting in front of Judge McNulty again. Tell them they have laxatives in them or something. Want me to write that on there in Sharpie?"

"He'd probably want to eat them then. It might help remove the stick from his butt."

We both laugh, and I take the pan of brownies into the kitchen, pushing them into the back of her refrigerator behind old butter tubs and a jar of olives. At the last moment, I stop and pull the pan out. I search through the cabinets until I find a small plate. Cutting a small piece for her, I replace the pan and walk the brownie out to her. "This will help with any mild pain, but it will certainly help with nausea."

Nola enthusiastically takes the plate and immediately takes a small bite, chewing a little before forcing the swallow down. She looks up at the ceiling and sighs. "I wish I had the appetite to eat the whole pan."

"Definitely don't do that," I chuckle.

"You have a gift. This is the best brownie I've ever tasted, and even my taste buds haven't been working properly."

I pat her shoulder and walk to the door. "I hope they make you feel better, Nola. You deserve that. If you want, I can bring you more books next week."

She smiles and waves as I open the door. "Stay out of trouble," she says. "Don't go to any donkey shows." I freeze and turn around as she laughs and wipes her mouth with a nearby paper towel. "Yeah, I looked that up. Kind of wish I didn't."

Chapter 22

LIAM

"Tomorrow night," Chase says, closing his laptop. "Did you get the email from the chief?"

I pump my fists in the air. "Fuck, yes. Saw it a few minutes ago. We're going to nail Lambert. What team are we going in with?"

"Cooper and Resnick. Both great guys to have with us when we're delivering a nice little package to a perp. Beat cops outside in case someone runs. The beat cops won't know until we go over there. Just you, me, Cooper, and Resnick know. Well, the judge and chief. They aren't telling anyone."

"At least they aren't making us wait a week to assemble and brief. Every time they do that, someone on the drug dealer payroll in this department gives them the heads up." I look behind me to make sure I don't have an eavesdropper. Chase and I are clean cops, but there are dirty cops that like a little extra cash on the side. "It's nice it's quiet this time."

"I think everyone wants this dick off the street. Hell, other sellers want him off the street."

"Them next," I say with a smile.

Chase and I have been pulling all-nighters, either watching the Lambert house or documenting everything into the case system and our own spreadsheets and documentation systems as we get everything in front of our boss and a judge. We've lined up witnesses that are Lambert's buyers and will contact them to see who turns on Lambert as soon as we have him. Our warrant is finally ready, and we're going in as soon as everyone that needs to know everything about the house and the case can be briefed. We're also waiting on Lambert's ex-girlfriend's information on what weapons are in the house and where they're stored.

Nervous energy moves through my body, and I need to do something with it. I need a physical release like running or fucking the shit out of someone.

I've always hated running.

Except for a text message, I haven't talked to Lorelei since court. I've been trying to focus, and when I'm not working, I'm sleeping a couple hours or grabbing something fast to eat on the go. I've thought about texting her with something witty or a funny meme, but the mental energy to come up with something witty that'll impress her just isn't in my head right now. The only thing in my head is getting Jacob Lambert in jail and his brother in a proper youth facility or home that can help him.

I don't know why it hasn't occurred to me to simply text her and tell her I'm thinking about her until now.

Will she think it's corny of me to text and tell her I'm busy but can't wait to see her? She didn't tell me goodbye at court, and I'm unsure if she's mad about something that happened there. I did my best to not ruin her, and I'm sure she didn't want to act like we have a relationship in front of her lawyer.

What *is* our relationship?

I reach for my phone to text her, but it rings in my hand instead. The picture of Mom and me at a community park concert last year comes up on my screen, and I slide the button to answer it. I've also been unintentionally ignoring her.

"Hi, sweetheart," my mother says, her face filling the screen when I answer the Facetime call. "Bad time?"

Do her cheeks look pinker? "It's fine. I have some downtime since we got some good news. Do you need groceries? Want me to get you some books and bring them over?"

"Not necessary. I got some new ones."

"Did the library finally take you off the waiting list for the delivery service?" I ask, wondering if my mother felt better today and went to get her own books. She shouldn't be feeling that well a few days after chemo. She doesn't usually start feeling better until a day before the next damn appointment.

"Nope. That lovely Lorelei girl of yours brought me some."

I suck in a breath. "You've seen Lorelei?"

Chase raises his eyebrows across from me, probably also confused that Lorelei is visiting my mother. Normally, I would be concerned or worried that a woman I like stopped over and talked to Mom. Did they talk about me? But there's something comforting about Lorelei spending time with my mother if I can't. Lorelei would make sure my mother is comfortable and the house doesn't get too crazy.

"Don't worry. We didn't talk about you...much," Mom says. "We talked about dirty books. You want to come over and eat? I made a big pot of stew and had two bowls. It's good stuff."

I smile a little, and tears prick my eyes. "You felt like eating so soon after a chemo session? I usually have to force you to sip some Ensure. Are you sure they gave you the right meds and not a placebo?"

Mom looks away, and I know she's hiding something. She puts on a fake smile and shakes her head. "Don't shit on my miracle. You coming over or not?"

Thanks to traffic, I roll into Mom's driveway an hour later, surprised to find Mom standing at the door and waving like she was watching for me from the window. As I walk up the sidewalk, she practically bounces on her toes.

"I haven't seen you move like this for months. What's up?" I ask.

Her eyes widen, and she stops bouncing. If anything, she slouches and diminishes before my eyes. "I don't know what you're talking about. I'm clearly sick."

"Don't bullshit me, Mom," I say, opening the screen door and holding it for her to pass by. I catch a whiff of her soap. Mom hasn't bathed without the help of a home health nurse because she's been too weak to stand in the shower, and I'm worried she'll fall getting in and out of the tub. The nurse only comes every other day, and today isn't a visit day. "Did you shower?"

"I did for a whole three minutes. It's enough to wash all the important stuff. You want stew or not?"

"I'll get it," I say, directing her to the couch.

She immediately slaps my hand away. "Liam, I feel fine today. Let me try to be back to my normal self."

"I'm just surprised, Mom. It's out of nowhere."

"It's not out of nowhere. I got my appetite back. Once I started eating a little, I started being able to do a few more things around the house. I actually felt like cleaning. Sure, I didn't get on the floor and hand mop it, but I pushed the Swiffer mop you got me around a little. If I can keep eating, you won't have to come over and help as much."

"Mom, I don't mind coming to help you every day. I just haven't been able to this week."

"I know, sweetheart. Let me get you food, and we can talk about your week."

"Sit down, Mom," I say. My stern voice silences her, and she shrinks onto the couch. "Save your energy."

She listens this time, smiling a true smile that reaches her eyes. She smiles whenever I come over, but I know it's usually for show. She's trying to comfort me. This grin is real, though.

I go into the kitchen and scoop a bowl of stew for myself and look around the cabinets for some crackers. Finding some, I crumble the crackers and taste the stew. It's a little bland, so I open the fridge, looking for the Worcestershire sauce my mother keeps for when I'm over for pot roast.

It's not in the usual place on the door, so I rummage through the shelves, lamenting that my mother hasn't changed her ways in regards to having upward of ten leftover dishes in the fridge at a time. I move aside a butter tub and come across a pan I've never seen before. It's glassware and has pink and yellow butterflies on the side.

"What's in this pan, Mom? Did you bake something?"

Silence.

"Mom?"

"Uh," she drawls, and it only makes me examine the pan harder. "No. That's some leftover stuff from church." She talks fast, and I immediately know it's a lie.

I lift the aluminum foil off the pan and tilt my head to the side as I wrap my head around the contents, it all making sense. I'd recognize the way she cuts her brownies anywhere because I've been obsessed with those brownies and the girl that bakes them.

I grit my teeth, and my lips curl until my nose scrunches. Fury heats my neck, and I dig my keys out of my pocket.

"Where are you going?" Mom asks as I stomp by her. "Don't be stupid, Liam."

Chapter 23

LORELEI

Bogey yips, circling my legs in excitement, and I take my earbuds out since he's obviously trying to tell me something. As soon as my ears are clear of Metallica, loud buzzing assaults my ears from the front of the house. No wonder Bogey is excited. Someone is leaning on my doorbell like my house is on fire.

"Coming," I yell, wiping my flour-covered hands on my apron. I'm sure there's some on my nose, too, but the person at the door is insistent I answer before cleaning myself off.

Wrenching the door open, I find Liam standing on my porch with an angry look on his face that I've never seen before. He takes a quick sweep up my body, and his eyes soften when they notice the flour on my face. He inhales and straightens his shoulders, putting his sour look back in his sneer.

"What's wrong?" I ask in lieu of a greeting. His face is beet red. Instinctively, I take a step back as he opens the screen door and stomps into my house. "You're scaring me, Liam."

"I'm scaring you? I'm fucking scaring you?" he yells.

"Now you really are. What is this about?"

Bogey bounces between us, happy to see Liam, and Liam completely ignores him. This isn't right. Liam loves Bogey and has never ignored him or failed to accept licks and puppy hugs as soon as he's in my home.

"You gave my mother drugs." He spits out the words, obviously disgusted.

My shoulders slouch, and I blow out a sigh. "I told her not to tell you."

"Will you listen to yourself? You gave an old woman drugs and asked her to keep it a secret like it's some kind of sick game. What the hell is wrong with you? Why would you do something that...that trashy?"

I reel back like he hit me. Anger burns from my feet like it's coming from hell itself and moves up to my face, reddening it. "Watch your tone. You're in my house, Officer Lane. Don't call your mother old. She has a younger heart and soul than her grumpy son. And did you just call me trashy?"

For the first time since he's come in, he pauses. He shakes his head like he's waking up, and his mouth opens for a moment, then closes. He sputters, finding his words. "I'm not calling *you* trashy, Lorelei. You aren't trashy in the slightest. That was a trashy thing to do. You gave her drugs."

I turn and walk back to the kitchen. "Show yourself out. I have the mixer on. I'm busy. I trust you can find classier women that won't do something horrible and trashy by giving your mom something to help the pain and nausea." I stop and turn to him, flashing the smile I know he likes. "How is she feeling? Tell me all about how I ruined your mother."

He flexes his jaw and looks at me with such disgust that my heart breaks into a million pieces. Even when we first met and he didn't like what I did for a living, he didn't look at me like this. He glares at me with disgust, and tears prick my eyes.

I turn away and stomp to the kitchen. I know he won't hit me or tackle me, and I fully expect him to leave.

What I don't expect is for him to follow me, Bogey still playfully jumping on him and trying to get his attention.

"I want to talk about this. Why did you do it?"

I get buttermilk out of the fridge and close the door hard enough that I check to make sure I didn't break the door. "I don't know, Liam. Maybe it's because your mother can't keep food down, and I have something that can help with that growing in my greenhouse."

"It's sick and wrong." He points his index finger. If it's possible, he's getting angrier the longer he's here.

I've had enough of his shit.

"Why? Because you say so? Because your moral compass has decided that she doesn't have a right to make medical decisions for her body? You treat her like a child!" I yell, slamming the buttermilk on the counter so hard that liquid comes out of the container a foot into the air. It splashes on the granite and soaks the front of my apron. I ignore it, letting the angry tears fall in front of him.

I don't care what he thinks. I've never let him see full tears before, even when I was in handcuffs. But I don't fucking care now. I don't often cry when I'm sad. When tears make an appearance on me, someone better back the fuck up because they only come during anger and frustration.

"I take care of her!" he yells back, pointing to his chest. He points so hard, he may give himself a bruise. "I'm the one that makes sure the bills are paid. I'm the one who drives her to almost every appointment.

I carry her into the house afterward, and I clean her house because the home health nurse does the bathing. I refill her prescriptions!"

"And you treat her like she can't make her own medical decisions because you have a vendetta against a plant! Just because you personally hate something doesn't mean you have the right to keep people away from it."

"That's not what this is!"

"Really? Because it sure looks that way. It looks like you don't like it. Little Liam doesn't like the big, bad plant that relaxes and helps cancer patients with pain and nausea. Therefore, he's going to make sure that nobody he knows and loves can get access to it, come hell or high water."

He shakes his head. "It shouldn't have been legalized."

"But it was. The voters legalized it. In a red state, no less. The people spoke, Liam, and you can't stand it because you're butthurt that the majority of voters want it. But it's against Liam Lane's delicate morals, so you just want to burn it down for everyone, not even caring that it can be a gray area."

His forehead crinkles, and he breathes out his nose as he grits his teeth. I'm on a roll, and he's going to listen to me. I walk toward him as I idly act like I'm stacking the plates I just got out of the dishwasher. "I believe there's a certain little medication that guys like when they can't get their dicks up. That's legal, but I don't think it should be. It's just not natural. We should totally crucify anyone that uses it because I don't like it, right?"

"I know where you're going, but this is my mother!"

"Your mother has been miserable and can't keep food down! I did her a favor. Sure, it probably wasn't the best favor, and I probably should have talked to you first, but she's a grown-ass woman. If she wants to have a nibble of a legal brownie in a recreational state, that woman is over twenty-one and can do it in her own home. What the fuck is your problem? Why do you try to manage everyone?" His eyes flare, and I step around the counter. It takes a lot to get me yelling, but I'm there. "You are not the boss of everyone. You are not your mother's boss, and you sure aren't the boss of me!"

He glares, and his lip curls as he steps closer. "Someone needs to be your boss! Someone should show you how things should be done. Fuck knows you're incapable of doing anything that doesn't involve getting high or getting someone else high. I'm surprised you even feed your dog."

Silence fills the room, and he backs away from me. He knows. He knows he's over the line. His chin quivers, and his eyes widen.

"Get the fuck out of my fucking house!" I say in a voice barely above a whisper, pointing toward the door. "Now!"

He doesn't move, so I pick up a nearby plate and hurl it at him in a half-ass attempt to make him leave and show him I mean business. Liam ducks in the nick of time and looks at the wall behind him as the shards of glass slide down. "You're psycho!" he screams.

"I'm psycho? You come into my house when I was just helping your mom in a legal way, Liam, and then you tell me I can't take care of myself or my dog. I'm so sorry she's doing better. And let me guess, she felt better after my brownies. Didn't she? She's eating, right?"

He looks at the floor, and I pick up another plate. "Get the fuck out!"

His eyes flick to Bogey, who cowers and whimpers under a kitchen chair. Dropping the plate, my feet move to my dog, and I wrap my hands around his furry flank. His ears go back, and he licks my face as he trembles. He doesn't like storms, and I guess yelling is loud like that. "Sorry, buddy," I whisper, stroking his head. "We're being loud.

Don't worry, the mean man will leave soon or I'll call the police to have them come get their bro."

Liam steps forward, his hands on his hips and a wounded look on his face. His eyes are swollen like he's holding something back. "Bogey," he mutters, seeing the dog so scared.

"Did you not hear me?" I ask in a calm voice. My voice is cool, but anger drips from my words, my teeth clenched and bared. "I won't take more brownies to your mother if that's what you want, but enjoy watching her struggle to eat or watching her hurt just so you can feel morally superior. Get out of my house, Liam. Don't come back."

He inhales through his nose and bites his bottom lip. He doesn't say another word as he turns away and stomps from the room, slamming the front door as he leaves.

Chapter 24

LIAM

"Get your fucking head in the game, man. What the hell is wrong with you?" Chase asks. He checks his pistol and pushes it into his leg holster a little harder than necessary before adjusting the Velcro on his Kevlar vest. "You've been weird all day. Did something happen with Lorelei?"

I shrug. "Nothing you need to worry about." It comes out as a grumble.

Chase furrows his brow and runs a hand through his hair. He knows something's wrong. He's my partner, and the way I told him to not worry about it isn't even how I talk to him when I tell him to go fuck himself.

It would help my mood for this bust if I had actually been able to sleep last night. I tossed and turned, unable to sleep without talking to her. I picked up the phone from my bedside table more times than I could count, my fingers hovering over her name on my contact list.

Her face when I called what she did trashy – I may as well have torn a ball off myself. It hurt that I made her feel that way. She's not trashy. In my anger, I just thought it was trashy to leave my mother weed-baked goods. The more I get to know Lorelei, the more I would never want to hurt her. She's too precious. Too gentle and kind. Too sexy for words. The hurt I saw on her face was the low point of my life, and I'm the first to admit that I'm usually harder on myself than I should be.

I've had a lot of low points.

And the comment about Bogey was way out of line. I don't think Lorelei's a shitty dog owner. I think she's an amazing pet parent. I think she's amazing in general. I was just mad that Mom ate Lorelei's brownies.

I sure as shit couldn't admit that Lorelei had some good points last night.

Mom was in a good mood last night, eating, and had some color in her cheeks. Should I look away from the drug usage for her sake?

One thing I'm sure of is that I should apologize to Lorelei. I should go over there, take her flowers, and tell her I'm sorry. A little voice in my head whispers that I should go ahead and tell her that I love her. I push that voice down because she won't accept it after last night. What kind of maniac barges in and says the things I did and then comes back the next day to profess his love?

No. I can't see her today. I need to wait a few days until everything blows over. Hopefully, I'll have had a chance to sleep by then. She'll be cooled off, and we can talk like adults.

It'll be fine.

But why does it feel like it won't be fine? Something about it feels so final.

I can't think about this right now. I have a house to bust, a meth dealer to charge, and a case to finish. Personally, I can't wait to hand this over to the prosecutor now and move on to the next scumbag.

"I think I do need to worry," Chase says, pulling me out of my guilty thoughts. "In case you don't know where you are, we're about to walk into a drug dealer's house without any idea of what we're walking into, and you just put your Kevlar on backward."

I look down and undo the vest from around my body, turning it around in silence. "I'll be fine. I need a cup of coffee and some adrenaline. I got this. We got this. Lambert's ex said he has a couple of pistols. Chief wouldn't even give us SWAT since other dealers get a magical heads up when they've done that lately." I waffle my head back and forth. "Until they find their leak on SWAT, we're it."

Chase scoffs, pulls my pistol from my own leg holster, and checks my magazine for me, pushing the magazine back into the weapon with a click before he puts the weapon back in my holster.

I shut my locker and glare at him before he can reach for my shoulder holster weapons. "I'm not a rookie. I know how to handle my service piece."

"Just checking," he says, not even making our usual inside, juvenile joke about handling our service pieces. "I don't know what's going on, Liam, but this is life or death for both of us. Nobody would miss us, but Cooper and Resnik have families, so get your head out of your ass."

I nod and exhale. It won't help anything if I get nasty with my partner and best friend. It'll just heap on more guilt and add someone to apologize to. "Let's do the thing, then. You ready?"

We move in silence up to the porch, our black outfits camouflaging us in the lack of moonlight. The fact that it's a new moon tonight was one reason we pushed to hurry the warrant through. A simple call to the utility works has the streetlight across the street on the fritz. Our eyes adjust quickly to the darkness, but anyone looking out a window would be hard-pressed to see us as we temporarily duck behind the bushes until Cooper and Resnik get into position at the back of the house.

Our watches are synced, and we have a timer set. When it goes off, we'll go in simultaneously. Our warrant is no-knock, and Jacob's ex-girlfriend had an old key. Resnik and Chase both have copies of the key in their hands, and we hope Jacob isn't smart enough to have changed the locks. He's exceptionally smart, but my impression of him is that he's trusting of anyone he lets close, even if they're no longer close.

Everyone has their weakness.

The timer pings on our watches, and we move, Chase ahead of me as he makes short work of the lock. I have my gun drawn and cover Chase as he pushes the door open. I wait a beat for him to draw his weapon, and we hear the backdoor open at the same time. A quick look to the back of the house shows me Resnik and Cooper have their weapons drawn and are sweeping the kitchen. Chase sweeps the living room, and I nod at Cooper.

We don't announce ourselves as we move through the main level. There's a basement where Carlton sleeps, according to the ex-girlfriend, and an upstairs where Lambert sleeps. Both need to be cleared.

The sound of tires on the gravel outside indicates the beat cops are on the street to catch anyone we miss if they run or if Carlton bolts from the sliding door entrance to the basement.

I put up a fist, stopping Chase and getting Cooper's attention. Once I have eye contact with Cooper, I point to him and Resnik and point to the basement. They can get Carlton.

Chase and I move up the stairs in perfect academy training formation. My pistol is up and pointing to the top of the stairs while Chase brings up the rear, pointing his weapon to the landing on the other side of the stairs.

It's obvious everyone in the house is sleeping.

Not for long.

Commotion comes from the basement, and Carlton lets out a muffled scream. Lambert must be a light sleeper or actually awake because he mutters a cuss word in the far bedroom as Chase and I haul ass up the stairs.

But we're not fast enough.

Shots ring out as Jacob Lambert appears in the doorway. His short blond hair is rumpled, and his small gold earrings shine in the dim light coming from a lamp in his room. His t-shirt is dirty, and he's wearing black underwear that only enhances his pale skin. He's the stereotypical picture of every man arrested in the middle of the night.

"Move!" I say, pushing Chase through the hall bathroom door just in time.

I dive toward a guest room door across the hall from the bathroom, but it's locked. A stinging pain rips through my left shoulder, and somewhere in the hubbub Chase screams my name as I fall back against the guest room door.

Chase shoots. At least, I think it's Chase. Bullets ping back and forth as I stay against the wall, dragging myself along the hallway. Thankfully, Lambert ducks behind his bedroom door to avoid Chase's bullets. He must see Chase as the bigger threat and aims toward the bathroom with most shots.

"Liam! Status!" Chase yells, clearing his magazine and reloading. The sound of his used magazine hitting the floor and Chase's heavy breathing is somehow comforting. It's only because I know him so well that I hear even a glimmer of panic in his voice.

"I'm hit but fine. It's just a scratch. Stay where you are."

I roll my shoulder a bit. It may be just a scratch, but it's bleeding like a stuck pig. I can't deal with that now because shots come from the basement. Chase and I look at each other with wide eyes. I hope those bullets aren't in Resnik or Cooper. I also hope they aren't in Carlton since he's just a teenager, but I also want my guys to go home.

"Jacob, this house is surrounded if you check your window. You aren't getting out of here," Chase says. "We have a warrant for your arrest for drug trafficking, possession, drug manufacturing, possession with intent to sell, felony weapons violations, and probably a few I'll have to look up when we read your rights. Not to mention you shot at police officers and injured one. Put the weapon down and come out of your room."

"Fuck you, pig!"

Why do criminals call *every* cop a pig? I work out and only eat one doughnut a month. It's really hurtful.

"Drop the weapon and slide it out of the room."

Jacob's response is to fire two bullets through the wall in protest. At least that's two fewer bullets he has in the gun.

Chase sticks his head out of the bathroom, and I wave him back. I point to the room, and he shakes his head at me. He knows I'm going in alone. I can't risk us both being shot. There's another scuffle coming from outside at the front of the house. Carlton must be out there with the police, and I count on that noise distracting Jacob enough so he'll look out the window.

I make my move, pushing through the doorway just as Jacob fires another shot. The bullet grazes my arm a little lower than the first one, and I duck behind the bed, lift my weapon, and blindly shoot. I normally wouldn't attempt that without knowing exactly where every person in the house is, but I know Chase is still taking cover.

Jacob curses and goes down with a loud grunt. My cop instincts won't let me trust him, though. I commando crawl around the side of the bed and peek around the corner of the box springs. Jacob is on the floor, and I point my gun at him again, hoping he's down for the count.

"What's happening?" Chase yells.

"Suspect down. Stay where you are," I say calmly.

I creep over to where Jacob is spread eagle on the floor, a wound in his leg.

Fuck, he shouldn't be out with a leg wound, especially if I didn't get the artery. He knows I know he's faking, and he slams the door with his foot before I can get my hand on it. He comes off the floor, throws his fist, and knocks my gun to the floor.

He's fast. Too fast. His movements aren't that of a normal human, even one on an adrenaline rush because the police came into his house. Something is wrong with the way he's moving. It's jerky and faster than me, and I'm quick.

"Liam!" Chase yells, coming down the hall just in time for Jacob to reach up and lock the bedroom door, Chase not getting a clear shot.

Chase immediately starts shouldering the door, ready to come in.

I have more important concerns. I have no gun, and I need to make sure Lambert doesn't either. He must have dropped it when I got him in the leg.

Sirens approach outside, and I know there's an ambulance here for someone. Hopefully, they won't have to call the morgue for me.

Parts of the door splinter, and Chase furiously kicks and punches at the door as he tries to get to me. Jacob ignores it and hastily searches the room for his gun until I sweep his legs under him.

The problem with Jacob Lambert is his size. He may be the first perp I've tangled with that's bigger than me. He's built like an MMA fighter with two inches on my height. I'm no slouch and can hold my own, but his preferred workout is boxing, while mine is swimming laps and tennis.

In the absence of our weapons, fists have to do.

I take a swing at him and connect with his nose. Blood splatters my face, his face, and the nearby wall. In retaliation, he lunges forward, grabs me around the waist, and slams me into a nearby night table. Sharp wood pokes through my side as my weight shatters the table, and even Lambert grimaces as I slide off the table with a chunk of wood through my side like I'm an extra on *Buffy the Vampire Slayer*.

I've never felt this kind of pain before. Adrenaline took care of my bullet wounds, but there's not enough adrenaline left to fight the pain from my side.

Wobbling, I manage to stand, which only makes blood pour out of my side as my peripheral vision is suddenly gone. A quick look down shows that blood is everywhere, and I'm pretty sure it's mine. It pools onto the floor and runs down my left leg. I can only see in tunnel vision, but I can see Jacob's hand coming toward my face as he punches me again like it's happening in slow motion.

I give it everything I have, but it's not enough. They teach us in the academy to stay upright as much as we can. If we go down to the ground, that's a different set of skills and not good unless you're a former wrestler.

I go down anyway.

A heavy weight settles on top of me. At first, I think he's thrown furniture on me. Then I realize it's his body, and his hands are around my neck.

Crushing pain moves through my throat and windpipe as he puts his full concentration into killing me. Fear grips me, and I force my head up, headbutting him in the face.

My attempt at protecting myself from being strangled to death is rewarded with a slap across the face. "You're my little bitch now, aren't you?" he taunts. "So, I'll slap you like you're my bitch. Thought you could come in my house and fuck with my business."

"You can't..." I can't speak. The sound comes out as a squeak and requires air to finish. I want to tell him he's not going to accomplish anything by killing me except getting a murder charge on top of everything. Then again, he's going away for a long time. Maybe he thinks it doesn't matter. Maybe he thinks he'll be a hero in prison for killing a drug task force agent.

Pain is everywhere. I want to give up. I think of Mom and how I've been so worried about her pain, especially if the prognosis wasn't good. I was worried she'd feel like this at the end. Is this what it's like to feel so much pain you just want to die? Do you just want to beg someone to end it?

My side hurts, but it's nothing compared to my throat. I can't get air into my lungs, and my eyes feel heavy as blood vessels burst. At least, that's what I imagine is happening when my eyes feel like they'll explode or even pop out of my face. Intense pain and the sudden fear of suffocation move my hands until I'm furiously punching Lambert.

His boxing training must kick in. Or maybe he's just hyped up on adrenaline or his own product enough to have the strength to not be bothered by hard punches to the face. His blood drips onto my skin, and I can't think straight enough to think of something else to do to save myself.

All I can think of is Mom. How will she ever recover from losing me? She won't. She'll be alone.

Amanda. Something happens in my brain, and I hear her. I can't see her, but I hear her telling me to fight and survive.

I furiously claw at Lambert's skin until my short fingernails bend. It's like trying to scratch a tiger. At that moment, I'm sure he's taken his own product. Even with his build and boxer training, his energy is not normal. Our intel never indicated anything about him taking his own product, so this must be new.

Chase. I hope he makes it out. God, please let him go on and do good in the world if I can't. Protect him, and don't let him be too sad.

My vision goes black, and my throat feels like it's collapsing on itself. I can't think. Thoughts of Mom, Amanda, and Chase go out of my head as I sink into death.

A loud bang like splintered wood.

Shouted orders that sound like Chase telling Lambert to do something.

Loud pops like fireworks that make my ears ring.

Something warm hits my face, and a heavy weight settles on me like a weighted blanket. Death?

One last thought, though, and I fight for it. I fight for it because I want my last thought to be of Lorelei. I'll never get to kiss her freckles every night before bed.

Chapter 25

LORELEI

"So, why are we doing retail therapy?" Kailee asks, swinging her packages onto the extra chair near her at the table. "Is this about your douche cop boyfriend?"

I place my own packages from our shopping trip down at the table and sigh in response. A new pair of boots, new aprons from the kitchen store, and a new pair of diamond stud earrings won't make me feel better, but it's a start.

Nothing can make me feel better.

I was wrong. I know that. I should have asked Liam if I could take Nola brownies. He would have said no, and we'd at least be acting like civilized adults with each other, even if I think he's being a baby about something that makes her feel better.

I've been an emotional mess since the incident a couple of nights ago. Sleep hasn't come easy, and I've wanted to text him that I was sorry about taking brownies to his mother. It's just that I'm still mad that he said those mean things to me. I've hugged Bogey for the last two nights, worrying that Liam's so mad that he would call animal control and try to report me for being a bad pet owner. Most of that fear is my normal anxiety, triggered by exhaustion. I don't think he'd do anything to hurt me, and I'm certain he wouldn't do anything to hurt Bogey. The idea of Bogey in a cage at a shelter would kill me. Thankfully, I think the thought of it would also kill Liam.

I can't concentrate. I can't sleep, but I'm so tired that the bags under my eyes have bags. I make a mental note to buy eye cream while we're shopping today as the waitress approaches our table with menus and tells us the specials.

As soon as Kailee orders a buffalo chicken wrap with a Sprite and I order a bacon sandwich with water, Kailee shifts in her seat and glares at me. "Spill. You've been quiet all day. It's like shopping with a zombie. You didn't order wine at lunch like you normally do."

I stare at the television mounted over her head and lament the fact that the news is on. Isn't there a rousing golf match to show in this sports bar? Like I need more sadness and bad news in my life. I fumble with the paper placemat menu in front of me. "It's complicated. Besides, you didn't order wine like usual."

"My stomach isn't the best today. I must have eaten something bad last night at dinner."

"What'd you have?" I ask. "Did you go out without me?"

She looks at me, pursing her lips. "Fish from Bernatino's. And yes, I did go out without you. I just didn't think you'd think it was interesting to go out with the teacher I'm taking over for as we go over a few things. I'll be taking over her baking and pastry class at the high school when school starts in a couple weeks while she's having a knee replacement. I wanted to talk to you about it. It may eat up more of my time, and she'll be out for three months. I can still help on weekends, though."

"That's great. The pay is much better for long-term gigs, huh?"

She nods and grabs a package of crackers from the bowl on the table. "You're not getting off that easy. What's going on with Liam?"

I tilt my head to the side, temporarily jarred because she didn't call him a dumb nickname. This must be serious. "I drugged his mom."

"With what? Roofies? You roofied his mom?"

"Why does everyone automatically assume roofies when they hear someone has been drugged?"

Kailey shrugs, and I blow out a breath through my nose. "I took her marijuana brownies because she hasn't kept much down during chemo. Liam found them and went nuclear."

"How nuclear?" She grips the napkin so tight that her knuckles turn white.

"He didn't hit me if that's what you're thinking." The waitress comes back with our drinks, and I unwrap the straw. "He told me it was trashy and that he's surprised I can even act responsible enough to take care of Bogey."

"Way harsh. What a dick canoe."

"Do you mean douche canoe?" I ask.

"That too. Are you going to talk to him again, or is this whole fascination with each other done?"

My eyes burn, and I blink back tears. Even though I can cry in front of Kailee, I don't want anyone in the world to see that I'm upset about Liam Lane.

I miss him.

"I think it's done," I say. My voice is strange, and I clear my throat. "I threw a plate at him, and he called me psycho. I forgot that happened."

Kailee lets out a slow whistle. "That'll do it."

"I can't imagine he wants to be around me after finding the brownies and then me throwing a plate at his head. Granted, he stomped into my house with a vendetta and called me trashy."

Kailee stirs her drink. "Did he just think the action was trashy?"

"He said that when I called him out. Do you think I'm overreacting?"

She shrugs. "Only you can be the judge of that, Lorelei, but I don't think he thinks *you're* trashy. I've seen the way that man looks at you."

"How does he look at me?"

A faraway look comes over her face, and she props her chin on her hand, sighing. "If he looks at you with any more heat in those eyes, you'll combust. That man would do anything for you. He was probably just shocked and mad. Did he try contacting you?"

I shake my head and look up at the TV. A ticker is scrolling across the screen, and the local news is playing. "He hasn't. Nola said he had some kind of big bust coming up. I think he's been busy with work. I feel like, if he really wants to talk, he'll send me a text saying sorry or something."

"You're probably right."

Kailee moves the conversation to the new purse we picked out for her date nights. I try to focus on her words, but my mind won't move away from Liam. The waitress brings our food and sets it down in front of us, and we eat in companionable silence.

Kailee must know I'm miserable. She puts her hand over my forearm as we eat. "He'll call, Lorelei. You'll hear from him again. I know it. If anything, he'll come to the truck with his tape measure and try to shut you down."

My eyes flick to the news screen, and my raised glass slides from my hand, spilling my drink all over the table. Kailee stands up and mutters a curse, but I stare at the television screen where Liam's face is. "What the fuck? Kailee?" I ask, pointing to the screen.

Kailee sees the look of horror on my face and turns around in slow motion. "Holy shit. What the fuck?" She waves her hands for a member of the wait staff, but not one staff person notices. "Ma'am, can you turn up the television?" she yells across the restaurant. Unfortunately, no one notices except for a few patrons that look at us like we're crazy.

This is some kind of nightmare where I must be invisible and not able to communicate.

Kailee walks to the hostess station, but it's no use. I pull out my phone, and my fingers shake as I enter the website for the local news. I only saw his picture on the screen. No sound. "Please don't be dead. Please don't be dead," I chant.

My fingers won't work. I can't put in the correct website, and tears of frustration slide down my cheek. I can't think of anything to do next. Where would I find the information I need? Someone else has to help me because I can't concentrate over the panic. Sudden nausea moves through my stomach, and I think of Nola. I have to get to her. I have to comfort her if the worst happened.

Kailee's at my side in an instant, wiping my loose ponytail out of my face. I must have pulled some of my hair from it. "Let me help. They don't have sound in the restaurant. Let me look it up for you. We'll find out what happened."

I look back at the screen where Liam's face is still shown. He looks younger in the picture of him in a beat cop uniform. It must be his academy picture.

My legs feel like marshmallows, and I slide down to my seat again as another customer notices something is wrong and brings over napkins to wipe my spilled water off the table while Kailee fumbles with her phone, clearly giving up on mine.

She fiddles with it and eventually goes to the Facebook page for the news station. She scrolls until I stop her hand when the same academy picture appears. "Read it for me. I can't understand the words. I'm seeing the words, Kailee, but I don't understand them."

Her eyes move through the Facebook post, and I cover my face with my hands. "Officer in critical condition at Holy Mount hospital. It says officer-involved shooting." She scrolls down through the post, passing the chief statements. We just want information on Liam. "There's something about him in surgery. But that's all…"

Her voice trails off behind me as I head for the door, my shopping bags forgotten behind me.

Chapter 26

LIAM

This is death, huh? There's lots of beeping here, like some kind of heart monitor. Bright lights blind me, even through my eyelids. Are my eyes closed? Do we even have eyes when we're dead?

Someone strokes my cheek, and I recognize the hand. The owner of that hand used to do the same thing when I had a fever or threw up as a child. The one time I got pneumonia, that hand stroked my cheek the whole time.

Is Mom here? She didn't die of a heart attack when she found out I was dead, right?

Sudden horror fills me. I can't be dead if I feel emotion like this. I've never been one to believe that anyone really knows what happens when we die, but I've only heard it was good things if you lived a good life. I think I lived a good life. Sure, I loved a woman and wasn't the nicest to her when we met...or yesterday, but that doesn't count, right?

Was it yesterday I fought with Lorelei? Is there some kind of weird time continuum after death? Did I fight Lambert eight years ago?

I hear voices, but they sound like someone put a paper towel tube up to their mouth. Part of the words come from a masculine voice.

Forcing my eyes open, I instantly squint again. "Lights," I try to say, but nothing recognizable comes out. It's a squeak. A gasping sound.

"Liam, are you awake, buddy?" Chase asks.

My heart jumps into my throat. When my eyes adjust to the bright light, he stands over me with tears of relief in his eyes. Did Jacob shoot or strangle him? Are we both stuck in this blinding light parallel universe?

The lights dim, and I realize someone has turned them off from a regular light switch in a room with a regular ceiling. I turn my head to see around Chase's body and find Mom shuffling toward me, bags under her eyes.

"Where?" I mouth.

The pain in my throat is better, but so is all the pain. There's a dull throb at my throat and in my side. But nothing hurts like it did when I blacked out.

"Don't try to talk," Chase says, sitting next to me on the bed. After he's not blocking the rest of the room, I take in the hospital room surroundings. My sense of time must be off because it's daytime now, evidenced by the sunlight coming through the windows. Midday?

I have no idea what day it is or if I've been in a coma for years. Fuck, please don't let Lorelei have married someone and had children while I was out. I search Chase's face for signs of wrinkles or gray hair and find nothing.

Looking down, I'm in a hospital gown and have no memory of someone changing my clothes. My arm is in a large bandage, and I can't see my side. Tubes connect me to something, and I have a feeling it's what's making me not feel any pain. Either that, or it's hydrating me. Maybe both.

I shake my head in frustration. "What?" I try to say in my strongest, most authoritative police officer voice. It comes out as air.

"You're in the hospital. You've been out for about thirteen hours. Four of those were surgery. You were hurt pretty bad, and I'm going to give it to you straight," Chase says.

Mom sits in the guest chair by the window, pulling a hospital blanket around her. She must have been here all night.

"You were shot twice. Flesh wounds," Chase continues, ticking off items on his fingers. "You were strangled within a second of death, and your throat is going to hurt like a bitch for a few days. Thankfully, it's not permanent. The blood vessels in your eyes popped, so you look like a fucked-up horror movie villain, and you had a piece of wood a quarter of a centimeter away from your intestine removed. You lost a lot of blood and had transfusions. It sounds bad, but you're a lucky bastard."

I look at Mom. "Why?" I mouth and instantly clutch my throat. Fine, no talking. That hurt.

I make a motion like I want to write something, and Chase understands, pulling out his phone and handing it to me. I open Google Docs and start typing. At least my fingers work enough to type a few words at a time, even if they don't work perfectly. It must be the meds.

Text: "Mom, why here? You'll get sick around others."

Chase shows Mom his phone, and she chuckles. "If you think my baby boy is going to be shot and nearly killed and I'm not going to show up at the hospital, you're dumber than I thought."

I take Chase's phone back.

Text: "You OK?" I point to Chase.

Chase looks at Mom, and Mom gets up from the chair she just got comfortable in. "I'll go get some pie from the cafeteria. I haven't had a good pie in what feels like months."

She walks to the door, and I smile as much as I can at her walking unassisted. She has more energy than she's had since chemo started. Seeing her up and around, even if she's surrounded by people and germs in the hospital setting, lifts my spirit a bit.

Only to be crushed.

As soon as the door shuts, Chase's smile falters. "You almost died, man. I was so scared when I got through that door and you weren't moving."

Text: "Lambert?" I type on Chase's phone.

"He was busy strangling you and didn't hear me get through. Didn't even pay attention. I had no choice."

I shake my head. "Dead?" I mouth.

"I used my weapon. Yeah. I had to. It was you or him." A tear slides down his cheek, and he wipes his nose. "I shot him, and he fell on you. I had to pull him off you. I was so scared, Liam. I thought I lost you, you mother fucker. You weren't moving under him. I'm thankful the ambulance was already on site. I don't know if you would have made it if they weren't."

I motion for his phone again, remembering the scuffle in the basement and the gunshot.

Text: "Res and Coop?"

"They're fine. Carlton was armed with a handgun under his pillow. What teen sleeps with a gun under his pillow? Res took a bullet to the foot, but shooting someone must have scared him. We're all lucky bastards that the Lamberts never practiced actually using their guns."

I nod and blow out a breath. The heavy breathing stings as it passes through my throat, and I wince.

"He shot at Res and then ran. Cooper made sure his partner was OK and then went after him. Carlton ran out of the house and right into about eight uniforms out front. That was the scuffle on the lawn –

them arresting Carlton. He's at a juvenile facility right now and crying like a baby."

"His brother?" I mouth.

"He doesn't know his brother's dead yet. He's crying because he's a teenager in a juvenile facility with no parents to come get him."

My mind spins. There will be investigations, paperwork, psychological evaluations, and required counseling for all four of us since weapons were involved and a suspect is dead. We'll get through it, but I want Lorelei at my side. My hands itch for her. I want to see her. Hold her. I want her to climb on the hospital bed and wrap her arms around me, never letting me go.

I take Chase's phone again and punch in the only words I have the energy for since my fingers are starting to go numb: "Lorelei know?"

Chase shrugs. "The hospital took your phone and put it in the possession bag. I can get it if you want me to call her. Chief called your mom since she's your emergency contact, and I was already here. I don't know if Lorelei knows, but it's been all over the news. Does she watch the news?"

I don't know if she watches local news, and something tells me Kailee isn't a news watcher. She either doesn't know I'm here, or she doesn't care.

The latter thought wrecks me, and I double over in pain. It's not even physical pain. It's the pain of a man that almost died and the woman he loves isn't at his side when he wakes up. She's angry with me, but I wouldn't stay away from her if she was hurt no matter how mad I was. Lorelei could bake my mom a billion pot brownies, and I'd still hold her hand if she got a scrape from falling off her bike. I'd pick her up, throw the bike in the back of my trunk, and bandage her wound myself.

So, where is she now that I'm hurt?

I should have told her I love her. I should have sacked up and apologized before I went into Lambert's house. If Chase hadn't been able to get through the door, I'd be dead and would never have a chance to talk to her again. That thought, or the medicine I'm pumped full of, turns my stomach.

As soon as I can talk again and my eyes don't look like they're filled with blood, I'm going straight over there and making it up to her.

But how?

Chase pats me on my good shoulder and nods. "We'll get through this, man. You'll get her back."

I look up at him, startled. Is it that obvious that my mind is only on her? I shake my head. "Hates me," I mouth, and even my lips hurt now. I need to stop moving my mouth or any part of my body involved in talking.

"She doesn't hate you. She'll come if she knows. If there's one thing I know, it's that you two idiots have something special. You've both fought it and tried to hide that you're crazy about each other. I don't know what happened the other night, but I know that your feelings for each other outweigh any words that were said. It'll take more than a bad night to get you out of her system." He frowns. "Unfortunately, you have to stay here a week to heal. It's not even your torso. They say there's a risk of dying days after being choked as hard as you were. They want to monitor you. I'll get you anything you need from your house."

I suck in another breath. How is my throat feeling worse? My lips and upper palate hurt. I also took some hard punches to the face in addition to the damage to my neck, and my medicine must be wearing off. I pick up the tube of whatever medicine they're giving me and thump it with my finger. "Hurt," I try to mouth, but my lips are tired. I'm not sure if Chase can even understand what I'm mouthing.

He looks at the tube and back at me. "I'll go find someone to give you meds and find your possessions so you can get your phone." He takes his phone off the table and puts it in his pocket. "You going to be OK here if I'm gone for a few? I may get some coffee. I've been up all night."

I nod. I'll be fine.

I'll just stay in this lonely hospital bed, wishing she was here to hold my hand.

Chapter 27

LORELEI

I bypass the elevator and take the hospital stairs two at a time. I'm out of breath and have been since I ran from the Uber to the woman at the information desk. She could hardly understand when I asked for Liam's room number, and it wasn't just because I was out of breath. The tears running down my face and the hiccup sobs didn't help.

Whipping open the door to the stairs, I run straight into a strong chest and spill his coffee all over the floor. He stumbles to the side and catches himself on the opposing wall. "Lorelei?" Chase asks, ignoring the coffee puddle on the floor and wiping the hot liquid off his hand. "You came."

I shake my head, blinking. "Of course, I fucking came. Is he alive? Tell me he's not dead, Chase! If he is, you better just fucking tell me." I grip my hair and pull a few strands from my head, not caring how much I pull out or if strands stick to my fingers.

A snot bubble puffs out my nose, and Chase makes a face. He pulls a wadded-up paper towel from his pocket, and I don't ask why he has paper towels in his pocket. I take the cloth and wipe my face, grateful for the kindness.

"He's alive, Lorelei."

The world spins, and I slink to the floor. Chase's arm is under me, and he makes shushing sounds as he tries to pull me to my feet. "He's not dead," I whimper. "I swear to God, Chase, I thought he was dead."

"Why did you think that?"

"I saw the news in a restaurant. The sound wasn't on." I hope my words make sense. They seem garbled, relief filling every emotion and thought in my head.

Chase gives up on trying to pull me to my feet. He sits on the ground beside me, crosses his legs, and stares at me like he's ready to listen. I take in his outfit of blue scrubs and a white t-shirt underneath. "Why are you wearing hospital scrubs?" I sniff. "Job change?"

"After last night, that's not funny," he says, running a hand over his scruff. I've never seen him unshaved. "I came in with loverboy, and I refused to leave until he was out of surgery. I wasn't exactly presentable, so a nurse found some scrubs for me to wear."

"What do you mean you weren't presentable?"

"I had blood splatter on my clothes. Blood that wasn't mine. Not the kind of stuff you want to walk around in."

"Please tell me it wasn't Liam's blood."

Chase smiles a sad smile. "It belonged to the guy that almost killed Liam."

Heated emotion comes over me, and my face crumples. I lean forward and throw my arms around Chase, burying my face into his shoulder. He smells different from Liam. Like hospital soap and a trace of men's cologne. After holding Liam and being consumed with him for the last weeks, the feel and smell of another man startles me, but I can't let go of him. He saved Liam. "Thank you, Chase," I whisper. "Thank you for saving him. I can't ever repay you."

He pats me on the back, running his hand in a circle. "Actually, you can. You can go into room 453 and see your boy. Please. It'll be a favor to all of us."

I shake my head. "I can't face him. We had a fight. Did he tell you?"

"No, but I know something happened. He was off."

I lift my head and inhale sharply. "Is this my fault? Was he off because I kicked him out of my house? Did that cause him to make a mistake?"

"He was perfect as far as procedure in a no-knock warrant. We were the victim of a perp that took his own product and a shitty floor plan. It didn't matter if we had a hundred guys with us, the first one through the door would have been injured. Liam gave the guy a run for his money, but the guy was bigger than Liam and on something."

"A guy was actually bigger than Liam?" I ask with a chuckle.

Chase slaps his thighs and stands up. "Hard to believe, huh?"

I wobble a little as I stand, the fear and adrenaline wearing off. I smooth my hair back and use the dirty paper towel to wipe my nose again. "Do I look a fright? Will he throw up when he sees my face all puffy, snotty, and gross?" I ask.

Chase grimaces. "I should probably prepare you for what you're going to see." He puts his arm around my shoulder and guides me down the hall to Liam's room. "I wouldn't worry about what you look like, sweetheart. In fact, gird yourself."

Chase doesn't come in with me. He stays out in the hallway, giving me privacy to see Liam. The room smells of hospital-grade cleaner with a slight smell of rubber gloves and plastic tubing. As soon as I walk around the curtain between the door and the bed, I freeze and cover my mouth.

Liam is bloodied and bruised. His face is swollen and purple in places. He has an IV, another wire connected to something that I can only assume is his heart monitor, and a tube under his swollen nose. He's wearing a blue hospital gown, and it's pulled down around his shoulder where I can see bandages and a shiny substance surrounding it. Antibiotic ointment or something similar?

His eyes are closed as he sleeps, but there's a heavy breathing sound in the silence. A gurgling, like he's struggling to breathe. Pulling my eyes from his face, they move to his neck, and I hold my stomach as I turn for the connected bathroom and heave into the toilet. The bruises and redness around his throat don't nauseate me – it's the idea that he came that close to dying. Liam's in pain, and even if I'm mad at him, he doesn't deserve to be in this much pain. What kind of animal did that to him? Chase mentioned a dealer on his own product, but how did Liam even survive?

I flush the toilet, wondering if I'll wake him with the flushing sound. *Should* I wake him? I don't know if I can even go back to the room and see him. We're not exactly on speaking terms. I should simply wipe my mouth, turn around, and leave. He's alive. I don't need to wake him up if he's out of pain and sleeping just to talk to him.

I walk out of the bathroom and freeze as I meet Liam's eyes. His eyes widen when he sees me, his face flushes, and he grips the sheets. God damn, those beautiful brown eyes are red and swollen. I bite my lip and force my legs still because my legs want to walk over to him, and my lips want to kiss his face until every bruise is gone and those eyes look at me with kindness again.

He swallows, cringing at the movement in his throat. He mouths something, but I can't understand it since his lips aren't working properly. Glancing at the IV in his arm, I realize he may not be able to talk or move his lips because of the medicine.

He breathes through his nose, but his eyes don't leave my face. We stare at each other for what seems like minutes, until my mind wakes up, finally understanding that I'm going to have to be the one to start talking if we have a conversation.

I clear my throat and fiddle with the dividing curtain, more for something to touch or something to do. "I was at a restaurant with Kailee, and the news was on. The sound wasn't up, so I thought you had died. I had to come find out for myself. I also couldn't stand the idea of Nola by herself if something had happened to you. I'll go." I point to the door, but my feet won't turn away from him.

He breathes heavily, his chest moving up and down with the effort, and he shakes his head. Reaching up with a finger, he points to the floor. What the hell is he trying to say? Is he telling me to stay or go straight to hell?

"I.." he whispers, swallowing like he's gulping glass. He breathes like I'm supposed to understand what he's saying. His hand comes to his throat, and he winces in pain.

Tears roll down my face, and I reach behind me and grab some paper towels off the sink. I blot my cheeks in front of him, and he watches me with panic in his eyes. He's obviously still mad and doesn't want me here.

He blows out a breath and brings his hand to his throat, pointing. "Is your breathing pattern Morse Code?" I ask with a chuckle.

He shakes his head, ignoring my bad joke, and tears of frustration slide down his face. I get a tissue for him from the nearby table, tentatively walking over to him and handing it to him at a distance, and he immediately wads it up and throws it across the room.

"Look, you're obviously still mad at me about the brownies."

What was I thinking? I shouldn't be here. Not after our argument. Not after he told me what he really thinks of me. This is a man that called me trashy and said he's surprised I take care of Bogey. It doesn't matter how he looks at me while he goes down on me or how he says he wants to be my friend. It doesn't matter that his mother has noticed a difference in his attitude since we met. It doesn't matter that I'd give my right arm to have him sit up and argue with me just so I could hear his voice. He can't take those words back.

"I just needed to make sure you were alive. I guess I couldn't bear the thought of Officer Lane not in the world. You're fine, so I'll just go," I say, jerking my thumb over my shoulder. "I'm sorry that I woke you, and I'm sorry if I upset you by coming here."

He shakes his head like an angry child that doesn't want to take medicine. More tears stream down his face, and he opens his mouth. It's like a horror movie with someone trying to warn the female main character that the villain is standing behind them. He looks at me with pleading eyes.

"Just point to the door if you hate me and want me to leave. Give me the middle finger, and you'll never see me again."

He breathes through his nose and claws at his throat with his good arm, obviously frustrated. But he doesn't point to the door, and he doesn't flip me off. I stay at the foot of the bed out of his reach, staring at him and willing him to make me understand. Squeaky sounds come from his throat, and I look around for a pen and paper so he can write what he wants to say.

"What's going on in here?" a nurse asks as she comes through the door with a syringe. She's an older woman, but she looks strong and like she doesn't tolerate people messing with her patients. "Are you upsetting him?"

"I-uh, I don't know," I answer honestly.

Liam shakes his head at the nurse and clutches his chest. He moves his hand over his heart. What the hell is he doing? It's the universal sign for a heart attack, and I look at his heart monitor. If anything, his heart is pounding. It's like he's playing the most frustrating game of charades ever. I wish he'd just flip me off. Is he trying to torture me?

"I think you should leave, ma'am," the nurse says. "I'll call security if you don't leave on your own."

Liam shakes his head and pounds his hands on the bed as hard as he can without removing his IV. He winces in pain as the pressure from hitting the mattress moves up his bandaged arm. The nurse and I both jump at the violence, and I inch toward the door. "There, there," the nurse says. She puts her hand on his shoulder, and he moves her hand away, looking around her body to find my eyes. "Let me give you something to sleep again."

She injects something into his IV, and I turn for the door, not wanting to be in more trouble with the law if she calls security. Lord knows I don't need to fall in love with whatever hunk appears to remove me. It's bad enough I fell in love with him, only for us to end up hating each other more than we did when I was a simple pot baker he was trying to shut down.

I should go home, hug Bogey, go for a long walk, and try to find a nice man to spend my life with. I shouldn't give Liam Lane one more thought.

It certainly shouldn't bother me that he squeaks something that sounds like, "Ove er," to the nurse as I shut the door a little harder than necessary.

Yeah, Liam. I guess it is over.

Chapter 28

LORELEI

I should replace this soil. A quick look at the browning marijuana leaves around me shows that I've been remiss in caring for my plants for the past week, maybe longer. I just didn't feel like doing anything, even canceling a truck event Wednesday night because I didn't have the motivation to bake. I came straight home from visiting Liam in the hospital and bundled myself into a wearable blanket where I stayed for a few days, watching *Dirty Dancing* on loop and eating frozen pizza. Today is the first day I've washed my hair and come outside to look at the world. A girl's got to make a living after all, even if the man she grew attached to isn't talking to her.

I woke up today, brushed my teeth, and told Bogey that we've wallowed over Liam Lane enough.

I run my hands down Bogey's fur, talking to him and whispering that I'm sorry he fell in love with the guy, too. He rolls onto his back, the warm sunshine of the mini greenhouse probably warming his belly, and I chuckle as I scratch the spot on his belly that makes him kick his hind leg. I sing to him, humming in parts like I've done since I first got him at eight weeks old.

"You'll spoil him," a voice says at the greenhouse entrance, startling me so that I jump.

I know that voice, and I gasp. Whipping around, I squint as the sun blinds me. When my eyes adjust, he's there. Liam – in all his Liamness.

Bruises still dot his face, but they're yellow now and not the violent purple and blue of last week. His stance is stiff, as if he's still bothered by injuries, and he's wearing a neck brace.

He's also holding a bouquet of pink peonies.

"I thought they only gave out neck braces for whiplash," I mumble, not sure what to say or how to greet him. Do I hug him? Kick him out again? Let him talk first to tell me why he's standing in my greenhouse?

"Apparently, they also give them out to help you hold your neck up if it's weak from being strangled." He points over his shoulder. "I knocked and then heard singing. Anyone ever tell you that you have a decent voice?"

Bogey wags his tail and goes right to Liam. Getting on his hind legs, Bogey whines until Liam bends down and gives my dog the puppy hug he expects whenever he sees Liam now. I guess my dog forgives him if nothing else.

"Sorry about it being so loud last time I was here, buddy," Liam says as he rubs Bogey's ears.

"Are you sorry?" I ask. I tilt my head and squint. "Is that why you're here?"

"I, uh, went to the flower shop and asked the lady for the best flowers to apologize with. She said peonies are traditionally used after something shameful happens. I guess that fits."

I walk toward him, careful not to touch him or look directly into his eyes. I don't need to be sucked back into the Liam Lane beautiful eye vortex that will only lead to spreading my legs if he's amenable. "I'll just put these in water. Thank you."

I walk to the kitchen and feel him follow me, Bogey bounding around his feet so that Liam has to stop every few feet so he doesn't trip.

I grab a vase from above the fridge and fill it with water. As I shut off the tap, a hand covers mine, and the warmth of him burns me. He's close. Damn close. "Will you please talk to me?"

"Like you've talked to me?"

He chuckles. "In fairness, I couldn't talk to you the last time I saw you. God damn me, I wanted to, though."

I redden, realizing what I said. "I didn't mean the hospital. You could have talked to me before instead of yelling at me."

"I thought I'd get through the bust and then have time to come over and apologize. I didn't mean what I said. I'm so sorry, Lorelei. I was going to come straight over here on Saturday morning, but the bust went wrong. I'm about a week too late, but I hope you'll let me apologize now."

I move away from him and lean back on the kitchen counter, blowing out a breath. My eyes move to the counter across from me, and I wonder if he thinks about the night we used that counter. I can't even work at the counter without thinking of what he did to me there.

"I should have asked you before I took brownies to your mom."

"Yeah, you should have. But I shouldn't have blown up like that. I shouldn't have..." His voice trails off, and he crosses his arms and leans back against the counter next to me, both of us staring straight ahead.

"You shouldn't have what? Shouldn't have stormed in like Rambo and told me you were surprised Bogey made it out of puppyhood?"

"Yeah," he whispers. I can't tell if it's because he's ashamed of how he acted or if his voice is still weak.

"Are you OK?" I ask, my voice dropping to his level.

"I was shot twice, was impaled by some furniture, and was nearly strangled to death. My wounds are healing, nothing major was hit by the wood, and it hurts when I use my voice too much. I'm going to be OK, though." He turns to me, but I stay looking straight ahead. "I'll be better if the girl I have a massive crush on would forgive me for being an asshole."

"Anyone I know?"

He reaches out and moves a strand of hair away from my face. "You know you're the girl I have a massive crush on. I've had a crush on you since I saw you. I didn't know how to deal with that, Lorelei. Looking back, I know fining you and taking you in was some kind of juvenile way to talk to you without having to do the work of actually talking to you like an adult. I was afraid to fall for someone that does your job. But I did."

"You fell for me? You could have fooled me."

He furrows his brow, and I would slap his face if he didn't have so many injuries. "What are you talking about?" he asks, taking his hand away from my hair and putting his hands in his pockets. I hate them there. I want them on me, but I'm going to have a go at him first.

"I heard you, Liam. I heard you gasp in the hospital that it was over. You wanted me gone," I say. I pull my t-shirt over my lips so he can't see my bottom lip quiver.

"That's not what happened."

"Maybe you were so doped up on meds that you didn't understand what you were saying."

"I understood exactly what I was saying," he says, his voice squeaking on the last word.

"I heard you tell the nurse it was over."

He laughs. "Damn it, Lorelei!" he squeaks again, upsetting his voice further. It's still raw and weak, and it's obviously harder for him to talk when he gets upset. He pushes off the counter and gets in front of me. Too close. "I didn't say what we have is over. I tried to say, 'I love her.' The nurse eventually figured it out and went out to find you, but you were already gone."

The world stops. The house goes silent. Even Bogey sits on his back legs and looks between Liam and me, trying to understand. He's not alone. I'd like to understand Liam's words because they don't make sense. None of this does. It doesn't make sense how I can fall in love with a cop that tried to ruin my business. It makes zero sense that the same cop is in love with me.

"You love me?"

"Do you know what my last thoughts were before I woke up in the hospital?"

I shake my head. Tears prick my eyes, and my body shakes. "Tell me."

He snakes his arm around my waist and steps into my space. "First, I was worried about Chase. I was worried we'd both die in that house. Then, I thought about how nice it would be to see Amanda again if there's an afterlife. After that, I worried about Mom. She doesn't have anyone to take care of her."

"I'd take care of her, Liam." I blurt out the words, interrupting him. Part of me doesn't want to learn what he thought about next. "Just know, that if you're in the same situation again, you don't have to worry about her. I'll make sure she gets good medical care, eats, and has plenty of books to read. I may not be you, but she will never be alone in this world. If you die on the job tomorrow, you can die knowing that."

He sniffs like his nose is runny, and he wipes it on the back of his sleeve. "Right before everything went black, I thought about you, Lorelei. I thought about how I was so sad that I'd never run my fingers through your hair again. I was sad I'd never hear you fight with me again, and that I wouldn't be able to kiss your freckles every night before bed for the rest of my life." He takes a deep breath and puts my hand over his chest. His heart pounds against my palm. "Because I really want to kiss those freckles for however long you'll find it in your heart to tolerate me."

I fist his t-shirt and bury my face in his familiar chest, sobbing and sniffing. I cry that we had to meet and dislike each other for weeks when we could have been crazy in love right from the start. I cry for him getting hurt and me not being the first person they called because I'm not his next of kin. I cry because I've never wanted to be someone's next of kin before, and I *really* want to be his.

I want him in every crevice of my life. My home. Part ownership of my dog. Definitely my body. I'll even let him hold the remote. He can have it all because he already has my heart.

"What do you want from this?"

He tilts my chin up with his index finger. "You. Just you, Lorelei."

"You have to let me have my job and not belittle me for it. It can't be an issue between us anymore, no matter how much you dislike it."

"Done."

"You can't handcuff me anymore."

"Are you sure we can't do that just for fun?" he says with a smirk.

I playfully nudge his good shoulder, and he pushes his forehead to mine, a serious look on his face. I close my eyes and enjoy the closeness. The feel of his skin against mine.

Back where he belongs.

"I want to know everything about you," he says, cupping my cheek. "I want to spend time with you. I'm off for a couple weeks to recover and go to mandated counseling. My days and nights are yours, Lorelei. I want to fall in love with you so deep, a backhoe won't dig me out."

"Is it going to drive you nuts being off that long?"

"It'll drive me more nuts when I go back and am on desk duty until all the investigations and psych analyzing is done."

"Is Chase on desk duty? I can't imagine he's happy with that."

"Chase is filling in for a school resource officer who's on medical leave for a few weeks. He insisted on doing something to keep his mind off things, and our boss thought it would be alright. It's not his dream job, but it'll keep him from riding a desk while the usual paperwork is pending. He's pretty broken up about seeing me like that and pulling the trigger on Lambert. Even though Lambert was scum, Chase still took his life. It's hard."

I nod. Even though they're both drug task force officers, I fell in love with one and owe the other one big time for saving my guy's life.

"Maybe you can help me bake while you recover."

"Now you're just pushing it, Ms. Rogers," he says. He smiles into my lips as he brings his gently to mine, his hands cupping my ass and pulling me to him until I have no choice but to wrap my legs around his waist and let him put me up on the counter as heat moves through my body.

Chapter 29

LIAM

Too much. Too much.

I set her down on the counter as pain shoots through my side. I pat the top of the bandage through my shirt to check for blood, worried I popped a stitch. Leave it to me to forget about my stitches to get laid.

"Are you OK, Liam?" she asks, running her hands through my hair. As long as I can have those hands on me, I'll be fine.

"Just a little pain. I forgot about my side." I lift my t-shirt up, and she gasps. She can't even see the wound – only the bandage covering it.

Her fingers trace the perimeter of the cloth, and a sad look comes over her face. "Do I need to kiss it to make it feel better?" she asks in a whisper.

"Yes," I whisper back. "But other parts also hurt."

She bites her lip and smiles. "What other parts are those, Officer Lane?"

I grasp her hand and slide it down to my dick that's already at stiff attention and wanting to play. I haven't had an erection since the bust because of the medication or the emotional trauma, but seeing her in person removes all of that bullshit from my mind.

She's here, and that's all that matters.

I stand between her legs as she sits on the counter, her warmth against my waist. "It's a shame you're hard. I'm not sure if we should be doing anything with you in a neck brace and bandaged all to hell."

"What's the matter?" I ask, kissing the tip of her nose. "You never get fucked by a guy in a neck brace?"

"There's a first time for everything. But, seriously..." She trails off and moves my t-shirt aside to look at the smaller bandage on my shoulder. "I'm not sure how I won't hurt you."

"We have to be gentle and not go at it like we really want."

"I thought Liam Lane didn't fuck gentle. You fuck hard or you don't fuck." Her eyes taunt me, and she grins.

My hand comes to her hair, fisting it and pulling it back a little, delighting in watching her mouth open as she leans into the hair pull. "If you make sure you don't push your leg into my side, you can take a ride tonight while I play the sick hospital patient."

She slides off the counter, grabs my hand, and walks to her room. Bogey tags along behind us, yipping and prancing like his favorite people are going off to play with him.

Oh, I'm going to play, but I'm only playing with his mom tonight. He only whimpers a little when I shut the bedroom door.

Lorelei's already pulling her white shirt over her head and shaking her hair around her shoulders. "Where do you want me?" she asks.

I take off my own shirt and pants in silence before climbing onto the soft bed and doing a quick bandage check. She waits patiently at the end of the bed as I get comfortable and remove the pillow from under me. It doesn't feel good against the back of my neck.

"Why don't you have a seat right here," I say, pointing to my thighs.

She climbs onto the bed so that I can feel her warm breath on my leg. I startle when she places a kiss on each knee, and she slowly moves up until she places one tiny kiss on the head of my cock. "Don't you want me to sit here?" she asks, leering at me.

"Not right now. I want you to sit on my lap and show me how you work yourself." Her head tilts to the side like she doesn't understand the direction, so I fist her hair and look into her eyes. "I want to watch."

I half expect her to argue with me, but she silently moves into the requested position and sits on me, her slit a hairsbreadth from my balls. I twitch at the proximity, but I want to draw this out.

"You want to watch me masturbate for you?"

"You say you've thought about me. I want to see how you've thought about me."

"What makes you think I rubbed off to you?" she asks, a challenging grin on her face.

"Because I sure as shit have rubbed off to you, and I think you've done the same, sweetheart."

"Show me," she says, her voice icy.

"You want me to show you how I've worked this dick to the mere idea of us being in the same room?"

She runs her hands down my hips, and I almost come from the feel of her hands in such a private place. Touching me like we know each other fully.

Intimate.

"Yes," she says. "And I want to learn how you touch yourself so I can do it for you whenever you want."

"Whenever I want, huh?" I ask, bringing my hand to my cock and gripping it firmly. I look down at it, and her eyes follow. "Can I get some help?"

She reaches for it, and I playfully slap her hand away. "Not that help. You have other things to do with your hand, Ms. Rogers." I nod at her glistening slit. Fuck, she wants me. "Spit on it for me."

"You are a filthy mother fucker."

I smile and squeeze her leg. "Get used to it."

She pushes herself down and leans over my dick with a look that I'm not sure is disdain or appreciation that I can be as naughty as the guys in her books.

She makes eye contact with me – defiantly not blinking – and spits down my length before running her tongue up the underside of my dick to blend the spit. "Happy?" she asks, getting back into position and moving two fingers to her clit.

"Fucking ecstatic," I breathe, working my hand up my cock.

I would usually close my eyes as I work my dick, but I watch her as intensely as she's watching me. I want to put on a good show, so I grip my cock hard and run my hand over my cock until the head slides through my palm with a wet sound. I'd normally be embarrassed, but it's her spit that got me here.

She works her hand over her clit and grinds into my lap, her head thrown back. A slight moan comes from her as she rocks against me. "I could listen to you moan like that forever," I whisper as I buck up into my fist.

"Promise?"

"I want to be the only person you moan for, Lorelei. Forever. No one else between us. Just us." I jerk my cock harder. Fuck, just looking at her is getting me there. Just watching her long fingers toy with her clit and watching her breasts move as her breathing quickens makes me want to explode. If I wasn't bandaged, I'd curl up and take her nipples between my teeth and flick my tongue over them until they were hard enough to cut glass.

I'm going to be a gentleman and wait for her, though.

I can be patient, but it feels like an eternity before her thighs clench around me in desperation. She shifts until she makes contact with the tip of my dick, humping me if she can't have me for real. She leans forward and grips my pectorals, riding into me as she moans my name and shatters around me, her hair spilling forward until it covers her face.

As soon as her thighs stop shaking, I stroke her hips. "Want to get on now?"

I don't have to tell her twice. She grips the base of my cock and impales herself on it in one stroke. Both of us whimper and swivel our hips into each other.

I grip the pillow at my side and arch into the pleasure. My side pinches a little, and I stop before I get to a full arch. My neck throbs at the movement at my neck, but I don't fucking care.

I don't care about the pain of my injuries. I only care about the ecstasy of her pussy milking my dick for all it's worth. She's gentle with her hands and watches where she puts her legs, but she squeezes her muscles around me and rocks down on me hard until I can't go any further inside of her. My balls tighten, and my vision blurs. I can't hear anything but the squeak of her bed, the wetness between us, and our skin moving against each other.

"Is my big, tough officer of the law putty in my hands?"

"Fuck yes, Lorelei. You can do whatever you want with me right now. If you want to off me forever, now's the time because I won't care if this is how I go."

I moan, not even caring when she reaches forward and moves a pillow under my hips. It's not the most comfortable position in the world, and I have no idea what this crazy, dirty woman has in mind. But I couldn't care less as long as it feels good.

I don't care one bit as she reaches around my ass cheek and slides that finger into the place she knows I like and rides my dick to fucking glory.

This woman is mine. Weed truck and all.

Epilogue

LORELEI

Six Months Later...

"Are you sure you don't want a clown to make you and Chase balloon animals?" I ask, stirring the brownie batter and swiveling my head around to see where I left the damn egg carton. Liam requested normal brownies for his birthday, his favorite of my baked goods, in lieu of a birthday cake.

"My birthday is no big deal, and I don't want you to make it a big deal."

"You don't turn thirty-four every day. You had a rough year," I say, nodding to his side. It's healed, and he and Chase are off desk duty, but he'll have a scar for life. "You're lucky to be alive and should be happy to celebrate surviving another year around the sun instead of acting your grumpy self."

Liam circles the kitchen counter and wraps an arm around me, nuzzling my neck. "I'm not grumpy. I have nothing to be grumpy about now that I have you. I'm also back at work, and Mom's in remission."

Not to mention he's moved in. His boxes still line the perimeter of the living room and kitchen as we slowly put things away. I've accepted more gray in my life, and he's gotten used to pink. He hasn't burned down my greenhouse like he once threatened, and I've become used to watching documentaries every so often. It's been easier than I thought it would be, but he still rolls his eyes when the weed infusion stinks up the kitchen or when he helps me carry pans of THC cookies out to the truck. He'll pinch the bridge of his nose or sigh heavily when he's annoyed with my business, but he doesn't say a word. He's kept that part of the bargain.

"Hello! Am I interrupting something?" Nola's voice calls from the doorway. "I hope I'm interrupting something."

Liam pulls back. "You hope you *are* interrupting us? Why would you want to see us that way?"

"Well, I don't want to see it, but I want grandchildren at some point. There are just certain things you have to accept your child does when grandchildren come into the picture, and..." Her voice trails away, and Liam cringes.

"You're early," Liam says, walking to his mother and taking her coat.

"I thought I'd help Lorelei in the kitchen."

"Nope," Liam says. "I just got Lorelei to bake for me without weed in her baked goods, and you'll talk her into putting cannabutter in whatever she makes me. You're a bad influence, and you two are thick as thieves. You'll gang up on me. Sit down, Mom."

Liam steers Nola to a nearby table and pats her shoulder just as Chase and Kailee arrive. What are they doing here early? The party doesn't start for another hour.

Chase and Liam exchange a wide-eyed look, and Kailee points her head to the backyard. Liam nods, and I freeze. "Is something wrong? What's in the backyard?"

"Nothing," Kailee says a little too fast.

"Nothing," Liam and Chase both say at the same time.

Something is definitely going on. Chase, Kailee, and Nola are here early, and Liam is clearly keeping something from me. His hands fidget, and he shoves them into his pocket when he catches me looking at them. Chase clears his throat and looks at the linoleum.

I slam the milk carton on the countertop and untie my apron, placing it on the granite as I open the sliding glass door. Liam is hot on my heels and grabs me by my biceps, spinning me around. "It's not ready yet."

I squint at him. They're not angry or scared I'll find something. If anything, his eyes betray laughter. His lips turn up at the corners. Behind him, Kailee bounces on her feet and silently claps.

I spin around and march into the backyard. Only then, do I see Bogey come around from behind the tree, pausing as he lifts his leg.

"For fuck's sake. I guess it's ready if she's out here," Liam mumbles.

"May as well, bro. We're all here."

Liam whistles for Bogey as I stand stock still, working my brain to figure out what's going on. There are no other guests yet, and the firepit we've set up for roasting marshmallows and drinking spiked cocoa later tonight is where I left it. There aren't any extra people out here. Nothing's out of order.

Bogey comes when Liam whistles for him, and only then do I notice my dog has something on his collar. A box is tied onto his collar with a pink ribbon around it, and Liam gets down on his knees to untie the box, patting Bogey's head in the process.

Liam gets the box untied and spins around on his knees. Why is he still on his knees?

Then, it clicks.

"Oh my fucking God," I say. My hands cover my mouth, and Kailee squeals from somewhere. I know Chase and Kailee are here, as is Nola, but I can't focus on anyone or anything other than the man I love down on his knees in front of me.

"I wanted to wait until the party, Lorelei, but some people insisted on coming to tie the ring around your dog's collar early," he says.

He looks over at Kailee, and she shrugs. "I'm excited. What can I say? It's not every day your best friend gets proposed to."

"B-but, it's your birthday party," I sputter as Liam opens this box. A tasteful diamond sits on a platinum band.

Tears well in my eyes, and one spills over my eyelid, immediately dropping to the deck.

"Ms. Rogers, you infernal woman that I once thought would be the death of me, would you be my wife and argue with me for the rest of my life?"

"You want to fight with me forever?"

"As long as we make up in that way we do, I'll fight with you until the day I die. I love you. I didn't know what love was until I met you."

I sniff just as Bogey nudges my legs like he knows what's happening. He's a smart dog. Maybe Liam sat down and explained the whole thing to him and when to encourage me to say yes by nudging me at just the right moment when I'm frozen in shock. Bogey sleeps at Liam's feet during weekend naps, and Liam's the one that walks him nowadays. Liam even put in one of those special fences for dogs that keep them in the yard so that Bogey can come out and play. A mental picture of Liam explaining the proposal plan on one of their walks strikes me as funny.

I ruffle Bogey's ears. He really doesn't need to worry, and Liam didn't need to train him to pester me about it.

I was always going to say yes.

I knew I'd say yes to him the first time my boob popped out when he was trying to get me out of the truck. Somewhere deep inside me told me this was the guy when he wrote that first fine and pulled out that tape measure.

Not that the tape measure in question hasn't made more fun appearances in the last few months. It's one of my favorite things to troll him with.

Liam patiently waits on his knees, which can't be comfortable in the cool air. I wipe my nose on the back of my sleeve and reach for Liam's face, cupping his cheeks and not breaking eye contact. I hear the clicking of cameras, and I'm thankful someone has captured this for us.

For our future children we want to have.

"Yes, Officer McHottie. I'll marry you. Did you ever doubt that?"

He smiles. "Nah. I knew I'd win you over," he says, standing and pulling me in for a kiss.

Chase, Kailee, and Nola hoot and holler as Liam and I kiss like we don't have an audience. More camera clicks. Clapping. In fact, we kiss so long, everyone goes inside and leaves us out in the winter air. Kailee mumbles something about showing everyone the video of Liam taking me into the station for booking at the wedding as they walk away.

When we finally break apart, Liam pushes the bridge of his nose to mine and exhales deeply. "I still need to get going on those brownies," I say, moving away from him, his hand in mine.

He follows me to the kitchen and wraps his arms around me from behind again, and I shiver with the desire to just be alone with him later. Unfortunately, I have guests to attend to.

He drops a quick kiss onto my neck, scoots my braid aside, and puts his mouth next to my ear. "Just once, wife."

"Just once what?"

"Put your special butter in my birthday brownies. Don't you dare tell a soul."

THE END

Thank you for reading *Contact High*. Reviews and ratings are so important to indie authors, so please leave a rating or review on the platform of purchase. The more ratings and reviews indie authors have, the more readers we reach.

Want to know when I have a new release, freebies, or promos? Head to my website at www.smuttybooklady.com and either subscribe to my blog or click on the newsletter signup at the bottom of the page. If newsletters aren't your jam, you can follow me on Facebook or Instagram at @authortoriross. You can also catch my podcast *Sitting Here, Reading Corn with Tori Ross* on most streaming channels.

...And I think Kailee and Chase have a story to tell. Stay tuned.

Titles by Tori Ross-
The Cuffing Season Contract
Contact High
Rocks
Winning the Witch
The Flower Festival Fling
All I Wank for Christmas

The Traveling Calvert Sisters (Romantic Comedy novellas):
Head Over Heels in Hawaii
Loved in Las Vegas
Christmas on the Cruise Ship
Out of Luck in the Outback
Turkey in Tennessee- Coming Fall of 2023

About the Author

Tori Ross is the author of several steamy contemporary romance books, novellas, serial fiction stories, and numerous erotica shorts under anonymous pen names. Her book, *The Cuffing Season Contract*, won the National Indie Excellence Award for romantic comedy. She's also the host of the wildly unpopular podcast *Sitting Here, Reading Corn with Tori Ross*. She lives in Missouri with her family and a dog that needs serious training.

Acknowledgements

Big thanks to the husband for putting up with me when I do eight-hour days, especially when I tell him to shush his stock podcasts when I'm doing readback. Sorry.

Thanks to my kids, A and P, for loving cereal dinners when Mom is on a roll.

Thank you to my dog, Meyer, for not eating my office while in the puppy stage.

A big shout out to my author friends: Selena Moore, Kelly Kay, Evie Alexander, Christian Pan, and Torri Heat. I can't wait to see some of you at events over the next year. Thanks for letting me ask stupid questions, especially you, Evie. Thanks to all of you for agreeing to come on my podcast so I don't have to talk to myself.

Thank you to Deb for agreeing to proofread for me. You always read my books anyway, so I'm glad I can put you to work in your new retirement.

Thank you to my supportive friends that always have my back. Some of you aren't readers and show your support in other ways. Some of you read less-steamy books and wouldn't touch mine with a pole but still ask how it's going. Others buy everything I put out. A big thanks to Jaime, Paige, Melissa B, Chrissy, Bridget, Lisa, Erin, Jess, and Nicole N.

A bigger thanks to Dainta and Linda for letting me work out the plot for this book over a drunken happy hour all the way back in 2021.

www.ingramcontent.com/pod-product-compliance
Lightning Source LLC
LaVergne TN
LVHW020344260326
834688LV00045B/1521